harlieTicket

Day

Gloucester

Massachusetts Bay

BOSTON

Ⓣ
Ⓣ

T T S

D

Plymouth

Cape Cod Bay

Sandwich

Nantucket
Sound

West
Tisbury

MARTHA'S
VINEYARD

NANTUCKET
ISLAND

ATLANTIC OCEAN

of Nicholas

$16.95
j/ARE
Arenstam, Peter
Nicholas :a Massachusetts
tale

Nicholas

A MASSACHUSETTS TALE

by Peter Arenstam

illustrated by Karen Busch Holman

 mitten press

A special thanks to Linda Coombs and the
Wampanoag for the use of their stories.

Text copyright © 2007 Peter Arenstam
Illustrations copyright © 2007 Karen Busch Holman

All inquiries should be addressed to:
Mitten Press
An imprint of Ann Arbor Media Group LLC
2500 S. State Street
Ann Arbor, MI 48104

Printed and bound at Edwards Brothers, Inc., Ann Arbor, Michigan

10   9   8   7   6   5   4   3   2   1

Library of Congress Cataloging-in-Publication Data

Arenstam, Peter.
Nicholas : a Massachusetts tale / by Peter Arenstam ; illustrations
by Karen Busch Holman.
p. cm.
Summary: Nicholas, a young mouse, sets off on a perilous journey
east across Massachusetts to retrieve a copy of his family history to replace
one lost in a flood, and makes new friends, has many adventures,
and learns about his state's history along the way.
ISBN-13: 978-1-58726-519-8 (hardcover : alk. paper)
ISBN-10: 1-58726-519-2 (hardcover : alk. paper) [1. Voyages and
travels--Fiction. 2. Mice--Fiction. 3. Animals--Fiction. 4. Adventure
and adventurers--Fiction. 5. Massachusetts--Fiction.]
I. Busch Holman, Karen, 1960- ill. II. Title.
PZ7.A6833Nic 2007 [Fic]--dc22
2007028855

Book design by Somberg Design
www.sombergdesign.com

Chapter One

A small brown mouse named Nicholas lived on a farm in the Berkshire Mountains. The mountains were very old and the farm was old, too. Nicholas's family had lived there for many generations, but Nicholas was just a young mouse, so to him everything about the farm was new.

The farm was nestled on a hillside in a valley near Stockbridge, Massachusetts. A river ran through the valley. The farmyard had a red barn that needed painting. The farmer and his wife lived in an old house with a kitchen garden out back. Nicholas and his family lived under the kitchen. On summer evenings, they could hear music wafting up from town.

The farmer knew the mouse family lived under his kitchen. His wife saw their paw prints on the kitchen floor many times. She asked the farmer, more than once, to get a cat to keep the mice in line. He would shrug and tell her they only eat a small amount of food and everyone needs a place to live.

"Nicholas," his mother, Marilyn, called, "you leave those ants alone and come in to eat." She stood at their mouse house door, shaking her head. "Look at him, Henry. That mouse could go all day without eating when he's focused on learning about something," she said, shutting the door.

"Oh, he's all right, Marilyn," his father replied from the kitchen table. "At least he is just studying the ants."

The excited mouse burst in. "Did you know that when one ant finds a source of food, he goes back and describes where it is to the other ants? Then the whole family works to bring it back to their home," Nicholas said. "Every time I move the crumbs around, the ants find them and lug them back. They are strong, too. I don't know how the littlest ants can carry huge crumbs back home."

"Nick, wash up like a good mouse before you sit down at the table," his mother said.

"Son, we have been waiting for you," his father added. "You know meal time is the only chance we have to all sit down together. Sit. Tell us what you have been doing all day."

"I did everything you asked me to this morning. Well, almost everything. I gathered some corn from the farmer's seed bucket," Nicholas said, hopefully.

"He will be planting soon," Nicholas's father, Henry, said. "The seed corn won't be around much longer."

"The corn was right where you said it would be, just inside the big barn door. I had to avoid the hens that were trying to get the corn from my paws. Then, I noticed a big anthill out behind the chicken coop. I started watching the ants and I guess I kind of lost track of time."

"Yes, you did," said his mother. "You were supposed to bring me some sheep's wool to restuff your pillow. I had to use dandelion fluff instead. It won't be as soft, but I guess your anthill was more important to you."

"Sorry, Mom. Tomorrow I'll gather enough wool to restuff everyone's pillows, with some left over to make batting for your quilt."

"Let's start with your pillow and we'll see about the rest," his mother chided. "Now, eat up. The farmer has been sending the sheep to the high pasture. If you want to get any wool, you will have a hike tomorrow."

His father looked up from his meal. "Just remember, Nicholas, stick to your task and don't get sidetracked. The woods run close to the high pasture, and I want you to stay away from them. That stand of trees is part of the old forest that covered this state from here to the ocean. Some of those trees were small when our family first came here many generations ago. They have seen a lot of history pass by under their boughs."

Later, while he lay in his bed trying to sleep, Nicholas thought about what his father had said at the dinner table that night. He wondered why his family had moved to these mountains and what it must have been like here so many years ago.

"Was there a clever mouse like me in that family? I wonder what adventures he had and what his life was like," Nicholas thought to himself. He fell asleep dreaming about the wild country long ago and the family that came west to settle it.

Chapter Two

The next morning, the farmer let the cows out of the barn. He fed the pigs and chickens. He sent Kit, his border collie, to guide the sheep to the big pasture on the hillside. The farmer caught a glimpse of a wiry mouse skittering away from his kitchen steps. He wondered why the mouse was in such a hurry.

Nicholas was trying to catch up with the sheep. Kit drove them along in a tight group. "Git along now, you girls. Shirley, watch out for that fence post ahead. Gladys, I won't tolerate any stragglers." Kit kept up a stream of constant chatter.

Nicholas climbed the fence post. As a sheep passed by, he jumped onto her curly wool. "Who's that back there?" Shirley asked, turning her head to look.

"It's me, Nicholas. I n-n-need a ride to the high p-p-pasture." Nicholas bounced along as he tried to speak clearly. " I-I-I p-p-promised my mom I wo-wo-would gather some wool. Do you have to go so f-f-fast?"

"Kit will be at me in a second if I slow down," Shirley said. "You just hang on. We'll be there in two shakes of my little tail," she added, chuckling. Nicholas did his best to stay on Shirley's back.

In time, the high hills and the old forest grew closer. As she slowed down near a boulder, Nicholas jumped off. "Thank you, Shirley. I will look for you for a ride back, if you don't mind."

"No trouble, Nicholas, but remember Kit will set us off as soon as he hears the farmer's whistle. He won't wait long."

"Don't worry. I'll be at this boulder before the sun goes down."

Nicholas had no trouble gathering wool. The sheep lost bits of wool all over the meadow. Nicholas picked up the stray tufts. When he had enough, he looked for something to bind the pile to carry it home.

The grass grew tall near the edge of the forest because the sheep never grazed close to the trees. He clipped off one blade with his sharp teeth and wound it around the wool. He needed a second piece to make a strap to carry the bundle.

As Nicholas searched, he looked into the forest and noticed a stand of oak trees. The sight of the trees reminded him of acorns, and acorns reminded him he was very hungry. He crept into the forest. Many acorns lay scattered on the ground, free for the taking.

Nicholas nibbled a bit of this one and sampled a little of that one. He worked his way into the forest, snacking as he went. He was very pleased with himself. He now had wool for his mother and a new supply of food. His parents would be so proud.

While he was thinking these pleasant thoughts, he felt a gust of wind. He tumbled head over heels among the dry brown oak leaves. Nicholas was frightened and bruised. Then, he heard a noise that made him shudder. He hid under a fallen branch.

"Whoo-whoo-who," the voice said. "What are you doing in my forest?"

Nicholas curled up in a ball. It was the great horned owl. His father had told him of an old owl that lived in the forest.

Nicholas peeked out from under the branch. "Please, sir, I didn't mean to disturb you. I shouldn't have wandered into the forest but I haven't eaten all day. The acorns were so tasty that I forgot myself. If you let me, I'll replace them with something from the farm. Tell me what you like and I'll bring it up here to you."

"Well now, whoo-whoo, you're from the farm, did you say?" The great owl ruffled his feathers as he settled on his perch in the tree.

"That's right, sir, we live under the farmer's kitchen. My dad told me about you." Nicholas worked his way out from under the fallen tree branch and looked up at the owl. "My dad says you are wise and know stories of long ago."

"Whoo-whoo, I know your father. I almost had him for my dinner one night. He is lucky, just like you. Your name is Nicholas? Whoo, is that right? He says you are full of questions. Whoo-whoo, well, are you?"

"I guess so. I like to learn about things. What do you know about my father? Does he visit here often?" Nicholas asked.

The owl sat so still that Nicholas thought he had gone to sleep. Slowly, he swiveled his head around and snapped his beak. "Yes, I could tell you some things about your family. I have seen many generations grow up here. However, if you want to find out about your past, ask your father about the journal. He keeps an old book with all your family stories in it. You had better be off, Nicholas. Your ride to the farm is leaving." With that, the owl flapped his great wings, took to the air, and was gone.

Nicholas heard Kit barking in the meadow. "Oh, no, the sheep! I've got to catch a ride with Shirley." He ran as fast as he could over dried leaves, around old tree stumps, and under brush to get back to the big boulder.

Chapter Three

When he reached the meadow, the sky had clouded over. Everything looked gray. Kit rounded up the last of the straggling sheep. Everyone seemed to be in motion. Nicholas flung the bundle of wool over his back. He scrambled up the boulder. He arrived at the top just as Shirley trotted by.

"There you are, Nicholas. I've been calling for you. I looked a bit silly whispering your name at each clump of grass in the meadow. The other sheep were beginning to talk."

"I'm sorry I'm late," Nicholas said. "I was eating acorns when I met this owl. I think he would have eaten me just as soon as talk to me."

"You should know better than to go into the forest. I did some lovely grazing today. I think the spring grass is the sweetest. All the other sheep agree."

Nicholas did not hear any more. He snuggled down into the wool on Shirley's back, wedging himself in with his bundle, and fell sound asleep.

Nicholas woke as the farmer guided the sheep into the barn. Kit wagged his tail and smiled proudly. He had brought the flock safely back to the farm. Nicholas rolled off Shirley's back, landing with a bounce on top of his bundle of wool. He hid behind a tractor tire while the farmer shut the door.

"You're back just in time, Kit," the farmer said. "It's starting to rain and, by the look of the sky, we're in for a long bout of it." Kit accepted the farmer roughly tousling his head as praise for a job well done.

When he got home, Nicholas had to tug on the grass strap to pull the bundle through the mouse hole. "I did it, Mom. I told you I would get you all the wool you needed." Nicholas tugged again on the blade of grass and the wool came in with a POP. Nicholas flew into the next room, rolling to a stop at his father's feet.

"Well, hello, son. Welcome home. How is everything in the high meadow?" his father asked. "I'm just home myself. I needed to take care of a few things with this rain coming. The farmer was out planting today, so we'll have some dried peas for dinner tonight."

"I gathered all the wool I could carry. Come see. I'm not hungry. I ate too many acorns today. They were everywhere on the forest floor." Nicholas stopped. He remembered his father had told him not to go into the forest. "Oh, I didn't mention," Nicholas quickly added,

"I met a friend of yours, Dad. The great horned owl. He said he knows you, Dad?"

"Yes, I know him. He is one of the reasons I told you not to go into the forest, Nicholas. Owls have to eat, and they don't care about family connections."

"Well, Dad, he tried to catch me, but he let me go after I told him who I was."

"It is more likely he had already eaten, Nicholas. But I'm glad you're home safely."

Nicholas's mother came in and shook the rain out of her fur. "Goodness, it is raining hard. Nicholas, I can see that you have been busy today." She squeezed by the bundle of wool.

"Mom, did you know the sheep like the sweet grass of the high meadow best of all? They told me so. I met an owl today who knows Dad."

"Nicholas, slow down a little," his father cautioned. "We'll have plenty of time to talk after dinner."

The mouse house was underneath the farmer's kitchen stove, and the heat from the wood stove warmed them nicely. Nicholas curled up, twitching his whiskers and licking his paws. His mother began to tease out the huge ball of wool into more manageable piles. His father paced back and forth, deep in thought.

"Nicholas," his father started, "a mouse is lucky. We can live almost anywhere and get along with almost anyone as a neighbor. We are fast and smart and notice everything around us. It is true that we have to watch out for some animals, such as the great horned owl. Because we are always wary, we see things most others do not. And when we see things, we try to remember them. For as long as anyone can remember, my family has recorded what we have seen in a journal. Both your mother and I make entries in the journal. We have not written in it every day or for every occasion, but we have tried to record the things that are important to us. Do you know what I mean, Nicholas?"

"I think so, Dad. The owl told me about the journal. Can I see it? I notice lots of stuff. Maybe I can write in it, too?"

"Well, for now, I want you to just know about the journal. I will show it to you some day soon. A mouse has to grow up quickly, and your turn to keep the journal will come along someday."

"Nicholas," his mother added, "all your brothers and sisters have gone out into the world. We have kept you at home to teach you how we write and to let you learn about the journal so that someday you can take over from us. Now, clean up and head off to bed."

Nicholas fell asleep thinking about the things his parents had said and listening to the steady drumming of the rain outside.

Chapter Four

It rained all night and all the next day. Nicholas listened to the raindrops drumming on the house's tin roof. Water collected in the gutters, poured out the downspouts, and ran into the dooryard. Little streams of water joined in the yard and searched for the fastest way down the hill and out to the road.

When Nicholas looked out the hole in the front of his house, he saw the farmer trudging by, wearing big black rubber boots and a long yellow slicker. The farmer, hoe in hand, made little ditches into which the water flowed. He scraped up some dirt, trying to make dams to keep the water out of the kitchen garden behind the house. Nicholas turned back into the house, looking for something to do indoors.

The farmer's wife passed by outside with her own black boots on, carrying an orange tabby cat under her umbrella. The cat looked as miserable as the weather.

The rain continued for the rest of the week. Sometimes it would slow down and almost stop. Nicholas would get ready to go outside and then the rain would start up again. Soon, he couldn't stand in front of the mouse hole that looked out to the barnyard anymore. The area was all wet, wet, wet. His mother and father had to move their belongings to higher ground farther back in the farmer's house.

"Can I help?" Nicholas asked his mother, who was dragging an old butter dish cover they used as a dining table farther back into the house.

"Grab those chairs, Nicholas," his mother said, pointing to some empty wooden spools. "It is still dry back in here. If this rain doesn't let up, we will be washed right out of our house." She moved the over-turned cover around, adjusting it to fit the new room.

"Put your father's chair over here, Nicholas," she said, pointing to one end of their table.

"Where is Dad?" Nicholas asked. "I haven't seen him all morning."

"He is worried about the journal. He wants to put it somewhere safe. Some place where the water can't get to it. I think he has taken it up into the farmer's house. He should be back soon."

Nicholas and his mother were settling things into their new locations when his father ran back into the room.

"Since when did the farmer have a cat?" His father was panting hard, trying to catch his breath. "I was looking for an out-of-the-way place to store the journal when I came face-to-face with a tabby cat! I think the cat was as surprised as I was," he added. "I had all I could do to ditch the journal and grab this cracker. Before the tabby realized what he was looking at, I was halfway across the room. He took two leaps and he caught up with me just as I went down the hole in the kitchen baseboard. It was a close call."

"Are you alright? Let me see. Did he scratch you anywhere?" Both Nicholas and his mother helped his father to sit down. They made dinner out of the cracker left over from the farmer's meal.

"You know, Nicholas," his father said, nibbling on an edge of the cracker, "the river, which can make this area such a good place for farming, can also be dangerous. The soil benefits from the water and nutrients brought by the river. However, when it rains hard like this for days on end, the river starts to rise. The wet, spring-time ground can't absorb any more water, so the river will overflow its banks."

"Because we live in a steep valley the water can't spread out. It just gets higher and higher," his mother added. "We have seen some bad floods in our time, haven't we, dear?"

"Yes, and this one promises to be one of the worst," Henry said. "All we can do now is wait out the rain and hope the river doesn't rise too fast."

Nicholas and his family made the best of their new rooms and settled in for the night. It was still dark when Nicholas awoke to the sounds of creaks and groans and a rush of water.

"Nicholas, get up quickly!" His mother was shaking him. "We have to get out of the house; the farmer's house is flooding. Move quickly. Follow your father!"

Henry was at the entrance to their mouse house pushing the dining table toward the door. Nicholas helped him turn the cover upside down. His father gestured for Nicholas and his mother to jump in. As the water washed into their home, Henry shoved the butter dish out the door, jumped in, and the three mice spun off into the flowing water.

Chapter Five

The three mice spent a wild night riding on the swirling water. Their butter dish finally ran aground on the hillside not far from the house. They landed among all sorts of things that had floated away from the farm. There were old peach baskets, a wooden rake, broken apple crates, and the kitchen garden gate. The mice dragged a basket up the hill away from the water. They climbed inside out of the rain and waited for morning.

Every day for the next week, Nicholas climbed on top of the peach basket and looked down into the valley. He could see the farmhouse below. The day after the flood, the water stood even with the tops of the first floor windows. By the end of the week, the river settled back between its banks. There were puddles and muddy places all around the farm.

"I am going down to the house," Henry said. "I need to see how badly it is damaged. I'm worried about the journal."

"Let's all go," Marilyn said. "We need to see how much work must be done to make our house livable again."

The three mice picked their way around the muddy spots. The pasture was crowded with cows and sheep. They all lived outside now, away from the flooded barn.

"I'm glad to see you're alright, Shirley," Nicholas said, stopping to talk to the sheep.

"Why, yes, I'm fine now. We've had a frightful time. I didn't think my wool would ever dry out," Shirley said, shaking herself. "Standing under a tree on the edge of the forest is no shelter, let me tell you. Gladys saw something scary in every shadow. We didn't sleep a wink the whole time."

"I better catch up with my mom and dad. You can tell me about it later," Nicholas said, running off after his parents.

They stood on a dry spot of ground, next to a pile of debris from the house. The farmer and his wife carried things out and added them to the growing pile. The mice looked at the farmer's house.

"How awful," Marilyn said. "The farmer and his wife must have lost everything."

"The farmer spent his time rescuing his animals and keeping them safe. He didn't even lose one. The house can be repaired," Henry said. "Have you seen that orange tabby cat anywhere? I want to look around for the journal."

"We'll all go inside," Marilyn said. "We can watch out for the cat while you search."

The three mice made their way into the wet house. The floors were muddy and the walls were wet. They crept along the baseboard, fearful of the tabby cat.

"Now, as I remember," Henry said, "I had gone through the kitchen and was just entering the front

parlor when I was surprised by the tabby. I was able to store the journal on the top shelf of the china cupboard before he saw me. I hope it was safe from the water."

They were standing behind the legs of the big kitchen table. "Look, there are cat paw prints on the muddy floor," Nicholas said. "He must be in the house."

"I'll go into the parlor first and signal you when it's clear," Henry said.

When Henry waved, Nicholas and his mother followed.

"There's the cupboard right over there," Henry said, pointing to the tall piece of furniture. A reading chair and floor lamp sat stacked next to the cupboard.

They could hear the farmer and his wife coming back in the house. Henry started up the cupboard and Marilyn followed. Nicholas waited under the chair, watching the kitchen door. When his father and mother were on top of the cupboard, Nicholas could hear footsteps coming down the stairs. He crept up the side of the cupboard and met his parents carrying a package wrapped in linen. The package looked swollen and waterlogged.

"Hurry, I think I hear the cat on the stairs," Nicholas whispered.

"We'll have to open the journal when we get back outside," his father said. "Let's get going."

His father and mother started across the parlor floor while Nicholas watched from the cupboard. They were halfway to the kitchen door when Nicholas saw the tabby round the corner and stop in the doorway. The cat spied the two mice and started after them.

Nicholas squeaked. He jumped from the cupboard to the floor lamp and felt it start to fall over. He clung to the shade as it headed to the floor between his parents and the charging cat. The cat plowed into the fallen lamp as the three mice ran for the door, dragging their journal with them.

Chapter Six

Nicholas ran from the house. He could hear the farmer's wife scolding the tabby cat for knocking over the floor lamp. His mother and father thanked Nicholas for his quick thinking and brave action. The three managed to get back to their peach basket home safely.

In the filtered light of the basket, Henry unwrapped the journal. A mouse's handwriting is very tiny. Even though the journal was small, it contained years of entries. Nicholas's father removed the linen covering and opened the leather-bound book. He stared at it for a few minutes, and then he sat back without saying anything.

"What is it, Henry? Is the journal alright?" Marilyn asked. "Let me see."

She took the journal from Henry's paws. She gasped and showed Nicholas. All Nicholas could see was a black smudge from the top of the page to the bottom. He took the journal from his mother and gently turned pages. On some, he could read a word or a date. But most were like the first page, just a black blot from top to bottom.

Henry sat quietly, then said, "This book has been in our family for years. Each generation has kept it safe and added to it. Now look, it's all gone. The old family stories are gone."

Nicholas looked on as his mother tried to console his father. "Henry, we are all still together. That is the most important thing. We survived the flood."

"Dad, you can tell me the stories and I'll write them down as you talk," Nicholas said. "We can start today—right now if you want."

"There were years of stories in that journal. I haven't looked at them all in a long time. I could never remember the details of each story."

Marilyn said, "Other members of your family, mice we haven't seen for a long time, might know some of the stories. Can we get them to send us stories to rebuild the journal?"

Henry looked at Marilyn for a moment without

saying anything. He looked at Nicholas. "That's it! That's what we should do. I don't know why I didn't think of it before. Of course, I haven't spoken to him for years. I don't even know if he still lives there," Henry said. "He is sure to have it."

"What are you talking about?" Marilyn asked.

"Why, my brother, of course. William. Do you remember when he came to visit? He was on his tour of all the New England states. While he was here, he made a copy of our family journal. He always said we should have a second copy for safekeeping. I am glad now that he did. He left with the book and headed back to the coast. He lives in West Tisbury, I think. We can get it from him."

"We have so much to do here," Marilyn said, gesturing to their ruined home. "I don't think we can make such a long trip right now."

"You're right," Henry said. "It is going to take a lot of time to rebuild our home. It will be a long time before we can travel."

Nicholas listened to his parents and thought to himself. His father had said a mouse has to grow up fast and learn how to survive in the world. Well, he was smart and could get along on his own. After all, he had scared off the cat, he thought. He did get away from that owl in the forest, didn't he?

"I'll go," Nicholas said. "I can make the trip for you. I'll find my Uncle William, make a new copy of the journal, and bring it back to our farm for you."

"Now, Nicholas," his mother started, "you don't know how far it is to the coast or how to get there. Until now, you never heard of West Tisbury."

"I can find out. You can tell me, right Dad?"

"Well, I don't know, son," Henry paused. "It is a very long journey. I can give you some directions. The coast is a big place. If you head east from here, you will run into it, eventually."

"I know I can do it. I want to do it to help you and Mom. You won't have to worry about me while you're rebuilding our home, and besides, I'll be back before you know it," Nicholas said.

Marilyn looked at her son. He had grown up a lot, she thought. She hadn't noticed how much until just now. Maybe it was time to let him go.

"You have to promise me you'll use your head. There's no telling who you'll run into on the road, Nicholas. Keep your wits about you. Remember where you're going and what you're after."

"I'll be careful, Mom. You and Dad can count on me." Nicholas smiled to himself, hugged his parents, and quivered in anticipation of the adventures to come.

Chapter Seven

The next morning Nicholas was up before the sun. His parents fussed over him. They made him a special breakfast of a few peanuts and an orange slice rescued from the farmer's kitchen. His father gave him advice.

"Now, Nicholas, not all of this state is farmland. You will have to pass through big cities on your way east. You need to be very careful," he said.

"And remember, Nicholas," his mother added, "when you meet someone along the way, don't let them sidetrack you."

Nicholas nibbled at the peanut, holding it with his forepaws. He looked from his mother to his father.

"Yes, Mom and Dad, I know. I know." Nicholas bit into the orange slice. His mother wiped some orange juice off his whiskers.

"Oh, Nicholas, who will take care of you?"

"I can take care of myself now," Nicholas said, standing up. Holding back a tear, he hugged his parents. His father cleared his throat a few times. His mother's eyes welled up and she held him for a few extra moments. At last, Nicholas headed out.

"Remember, use your head when you get in trouble and look for friends to help you out," his father shouted after Nicholas.

All morning Nicholas was in high spirits. He was on his own and he knew this area well. He followed the river and tried to stay out of sight. There were many animals out in the world that would like to make breakfast out of a young mouse.

By noon, Nicholas was feeling hungry again. He was far out of sight of the farm. He wandered along looking for some tender young plants growing on the riverbank. A mother mallard and six young ducklings were swimming in a wavering line on the slow-moving water.

Just then, they heard an earsplitting snarl followed by a high-pitched scream. Nicholas hunkered down in the reeds. Mrs. Mallard gathered her ducklings and swam out into the middle of the river.

From out of the nearby trees a tawny-colored streak of fur, chipping for all he was worth, blazed by and jumped into the river. Seconds later a spotted animal appeared on the riverbank.

"Ha, ha," the bobcat laughed. "That will teach you to disturb my mid-morning nap."

A chipmunk splashed about, barely keeping his head above water.

"I would jump in after you," the bobcat continued, "if I thought you would make a meal." Chuckling, the wild cat head back into the woods.

Mrs. Mallard swam over and nudged the floundering chipmunk toward the shore. Nicholas reached out to the animal. Nicholas heaved and Mrs. Mallard pushed. The chipmunk flew out of the water and landed on Nicholas.

"I'm much obliged," the chipmunk said, bowing toward Mrs. Mallard.

"Yes, well, glad to help. Come along, young ones," Mrs. Mallard said, guiding her ducklings down the river. She didn't like the way the chipmunk eyed them.

Nicholas shook water off his fur and rubbed his head where the chipmunk had landed. "I'm glad to help also," Nicholas said.

"What? Yes, I suppose I should thank you as well. I was nearly out of the water, though. Sure I would have made it. I never had swimming lessons myself, but I must say I did quite well."

"Looked to me like you were headed under the water," Nicholas said.

"Nonsense, I was in complete control the entire time. Anyway, I will leave you to whatever you were doing. I'm headed back east, you know," the chipmunk said, puffing out his chest. He headed up to the road toward the farm.

"Excuse me," Nicholas shouted. "If you are headed east, you're going the wrong way. East is the other way."

"I've been traveling for weeks now. I think I should know east from west, young mouse."

"I'm certain it's this way," Nicholas said, pointing. "I live in that direction," he said, pointing again, "and that way is west. I'm headed east myself. My dad said to keep the morning sun in front of me and I would always be heading east."

The chipmunk considered what Nicholas had told him.

"I still have a long way to travel," Nicholas said as he made his way up to the road.

"Now hold on there," the chipmunk called after Nicholas. "You seem like such a young mouse to be traveling on your own. What if I keep you company? You know, I can protect you from the dangers of the road."

Nicholas was doubtful. However, Nicholas was lonely, and it would be a long trip. Perhaps they could look out for each other.

"Alright," Nicholas said. "You can come along with me. But let's try and stay away from bobcats, what do you think?"

"Oh, that. It was a complete misunderstanding. The bobcat had no sense of humor. I'll tell you about him as we walk."

Nicholas smiled to himself, glad for the company. He was sure there would be no shortage of conversation along the way.

Chapter Eight

"We haven't been introduced," the chipmunk said, after a few miles. "I'm Edward. I come from a very old family back east. We have been living there for years. Perhaps you've heard of us?"

"Is that so?" Nicholas said to be polite. "I grew up out here on a farm so I don't think we have heard of your family. Can I call you Eddie?"

"As I said, my name is Edward. In the right circles, everyone knows of my family," the chipmunk said. Nicholas was beginning to regret traveling with this puffed up chipmunk.

"How'd you end up out here anyway?" Nicholas asked to change the subject.

"Funny story, that," Edward said. "I was after some cranberries. They have bushels of them where I come from. The berries I was after were on a truck headed to the western part of the state. Those trucks travel fast. I didn't dare jump off. I scared the dickens out of the grocery clerk when they unloaded the cranberries," Edward chuckled at the memory. "I spent the winter in the grocery store but, come spring, I decided I'd better get home. I'm sure everyone is worried about me."

As they talked, a red-tailed hawk trailed the pair high overhead. Edward showed off his throwing arm. He had picked up some pebbles from the road. "We used to throw cranberries out into the bog at the snapping turtles," Edward said, throwing the pebble.

Nicholas felt a chill as a shadow passed over them. "I think we should be more careful. Let's get off the road," he said.

Just then, the hawk swooped, his talons open in front, aiming for Nicholas. Nicholas made a dive for the tall grass near the edge of the road, but the hawk had him. He squeaked and struggled against the strong bird as it climbed toward the sky.

Edward took careful aim with a pebble, and let it go. The startled hawk dropped Nicholas and flapped off. Nicholas tumbled to the ground and landed in a heap in a clump of clover. The two small animals ran for cover in the forest.

"It is my turn to thank you, Edward," Nicholas said, when he could catch his breath. "I don't know what I would have done if you weren't there."

"Don't mention it. Don't mention it. I took a prize for the pebble toss three years in a row at my school,"

Edward said. "That hawk won't bother us again, I assure you."

"Yes, well, thank you just the same," Nicholas said. "Let's stay off the road. If we head into the woods, we can head straight for a pond that's not too far away."

The pair plunged into the forest, leaving the openness of the road behind. Soon, they no longer heard the river or saw the road. The sun went down behind the western mountains. Their shadows stretched out ahead.

"I think we should stop here before it gets too dark," Nicholas said. He looked around, unsure of where they were.

"I say we keep going. I have a feeling we will be at the pond in no time," Edward urged. He was anxious to get out of the forest, so the two kept on until dark.

Finally, Nicholas said, "I think we've been going in circles. Let's wait for morning."

Edward agreed. The two huddled together under a great beech tree. They gathered some beechnuts for their supper. They fell asleep listening to sounds coming from deep within the woods.

In the middle of the night, Nicholas awoke to the sound of someone tramping through the forest. Out of the dark walked a tall, bearded man with a saucepan for a hat. "Hello there, little fellow," the man said, tipping his saucepan hat. "I don't believe I've seen you on my travels through here before?"

"Edward and I are lost. We're on our way to Goose

Pond and the river on the other side of it. We have been walking in circles."

"Goose Pond, you say? I know where that is. I have traveled these woods for years. I can take you there." He picked up Nicholas and the sleeping chipmunk and walked into the woods.

"My mother called me Johnny," the lanky man said. "We lived in Longmeadow before I headed for the frontier."

He carried Nicholas and Edward in a sack hung around his neck. "For years I planted apple trees as I walked. I made a business of selling the young trees to people moving west. Of course, that was years ago. Now, I mostly help anyone lost, like you two." Nicholas, warm and safe in the burlap sack, fell asleep listening to Johnny's stories.

In time, Edward shook him awake. "Wake up, sleepyhead. I told you I would find the pond. Why, here it is! It was right in front of us the whole time. We must have missed it in the dark."

Nicholas was glad to see the pond and the river flowing out on the far side. He wasn't so sure he should mention their visitor. Maybe he dreamed the whole thing. Maybe Edward was right. They bedded down in the dried leaves and pine needles waiting for the sun to continue their journey.

Chapter Nine

The sun was well above the horizon when Nicholas opened his eyes again. He squinted, looking out over the pond next to where they slept. The dark green pine and hemlock trees on the far shore were reflected in the sparkling water. Edward snored steadily nearby.

"Edward, wake up! Edward," Nicholas said, shaking the chipmunk's foot. "We have to keep going. The sun is well up in the sky."

"Not now, Nicholas," Edward muttered. "I was dreaming of my soft bed at home and a big pile of cranberries for breakfast." Edward rolled over, smacking his lips.

Nicholas was about to shake the dozing chipmunk again when he heard a honk-honk-honk coming from across the pond—except it sounded more like hhmmk-hhmmk-hhmmk. Nicholas stood on a stone near the shore and gazed out over the water.

He could see a single Canada goose swimming in circles. The goose flapped his wings and tried to rise up on the water. Hhmmk-hhmmk-hhmmk, the goose trumpeted. Nicholas could see something was wrong, but he couldn't make out what it was.

"Edward, that goose is in trouble," Nicholas said, shaking Edward vigorously. "He seems to be caught in something."

"Now listen, Nicholas, we can't go around rescuing every animal in trouble. I'll never get home. I'm sure if that goose got into something, he can get out of it."

"I don't think so, Edward. Help me attract his attention. We have to get him to swim over here." Nicholas waved his little arms. They barely showed above the brush along the shore. Nicholas scampered around, holding up twigs as he went.

Eventually he found what he was looking for—two sticks, each with a bit of branch shooting out the side in just the right spot. Nicholas tucked the sticks under his arms and hopped up on the bit of branch. He was wobbly at first and several times he fell, but finally he stood above the brush.

He shouted to Edward, "Hand me that dandelion blossom. Quickly, the goose is swimming away from us." Nicholas waved the blossom over his head, squeaking in the highest pitched mouse voice he could muster.

"I believe he sees you," Edward said. "It appears he has a fishing lure wrapped around his beak." Edward began to take an interest. "I will float some of these

pine cones out on the water. If I lay a branch on top of the cones, it will make a kind of dock. We can walk out onto the water and reach your poor goose."

The goose swam over to the little dock. Nicholas and Edward could see that, somehow, the goose had wrapped the fishing line and a red-and-white bobber around his beak, one wing, and his webbed foot. The two animals set to work nibbling through the fishing line bit-by-bit. At last, the goose shook himself loose. Edward dragged the bobber and lure up onto the shore.

"There," he said, flinging them away. "You're free."

"Thank you so much," the goose said. "If you two hadn't come along, I don't know what I would have done." He settled his feathers and sipped some water to clear his throat. "The more I struggled, the more tangled up I got."

"I'm glad we could help. My name is Nicholas and this is Edward. We are on our way east. He is trying to get back home and I have an important job I have to do for my family."

"I'm glad to meet you, Nicholas. Thank you, Edward. My name is Alfred. Everyone calls me Al. Now, Nicholas and Edward, I think I can help you with your travels. I am headed north but I know of a big lake that is not too far east out of the way. It will make a good stopping point for me. I could carry you there and it would help get you on your way?"

Nicholas loved the idea.

Edward said, "Really, when I travel I like to fly by swan. Are you sure you can manage?"

"Oh, Edward, don't be silly. Al, we would be delighted to have you carry us, even part of the way."

"Great, climb up and hold on. Reach into the down feathers. Now, here we go."

Alfred beat his great wings and paddled his feet for all he was worth. Water splashed up onto Nicholas as Al plowed through the water. The two small animals bounced and bumped over each wave. As soon as the goose was out of the water, the ride was as smooth as downy feathers. Nicholas let out a joyous shriek. He had never traveled so fast in all his life. Al climbed into the sky.

"Eiyeee," Nicholas was so excited he couldn't form words. "This is the best. What do you think, Edward?" Nicholas looked over his shoulder at the chipmunk clutching him around the waist. Edward kept his eyes tightly shut.

"Just tell me when we land again. I hate flying," Edward said. His words were lost in the wind as the goose winged up over forest, farm, town, and city. They headed east together.

Chapter Ten

What would have taken Nicholas and Edward weeks of travel took Alfred only a few hours. He flew high over trees. He passed through fair-weather clouds. He checked his course using landmarks geese had known for generations.

Nicholas clung to the downy feathers behind Alfred's neck. He leaned over from one side to the other, looking at the view the entire trip. Rivers snaked

along through the hills. Church spires reached up to the sky. A ribbon of highway stretched away to the east. Edward kept his eyes closed and missed everything.

When Al approached the steep hills and water-filled valleys of the Quabbin Reservation, he circled down toward the water. "I'm going to come in for a landing," Alfred said. "Brace yourselves. It could get a little wet."

Alfred held his wings out in two graceful arcs. He went into a long glide just over the water. At the last second, he tucked his legs in and splashed down, sending water shooting out in sheets on either side of his wide body.

"We made it, Edward," Nicholas said, trying to wiggle free of Edward's grip.

"At last," Edward exclaimed. "One of the bumpiest rides I've ever had."

"We want to thank you, Al. Don't we, Edward?" Nicholas nudged his companion. "We never could have come this far without you. But, where are we?"

"You are on the biggest manmade reservoir in the state. This lake provides drinking water for towns and cities over one hundred miles away," Alfred said. "The area around the lake is protected and kept wild. Many animals live here. Some will want to be friends, some won't." Alfred swam along the shore. "Ah, here it is. Follow this stream. You'll find some shelter just right for small animals such as yourselves."

"Good-bye, Al," Nicholas said. He leapt onto a large boulder that marked the mouth of the stream.

"Yes, good-bye, Alfred. It was very kind of you to give us a lift," Edward bowed to the goose from the boulder. "I should think you would want to catch up with your companions."

"Good luck, you two, wherever you're headed." Alfred spun around, picking up enough speed to regain flight.

It was quiet now. Nicholas and Edward looked around. The reservoir that looked like a big lake stretched out in front of them. The tree-covered hills ran down right to the shore. Birds sang in the woods. Water lapped at the shore. The wind filtered through the tree branches. The sun covered everything with a drowsy warmth.

"Well, my friend," Edward said, stretching and yawning. "I don't know about you, but I could use a bite to eat and a long nap. Let's find ourselves some place safe to sleep."

"It does feel like summer here. The warm air and long trip have made me sleepy. Come on, Al said to head up this way."

The two animals discovered old stone walls criss-crossing through the trees. They ran up along the moss- and lichen-covered stones beneath trees of all kinds. Beechnuts, acorns, and pinecones lay on the ground among the dried leaves. They saw a patch of strawberries, red and ripe, growing in a nearby sunny spot.

They stood atop the wall, surveying the landscape. A whitetail deer walked out and drank from the stream. A flock of wild turkeys scratched at the ground after the beechnuts. Two red squirrels chased each other down one maple tree and up another.

"Nicholas, my friend," Edward said. "This place is an animal's paradise. There is plenty of food and water. The little hollows among the stones of this wall make an ideal home. The peace and quiet is just what I need."

"It is beautiful here," Nicholas agreed. "I don't know about a home, though. I promised my dad I would find my uncle as soon as possible."

"I know, I know, Nicholas. I'll tell you what. Let's stay here for a few days, just to rest up. What do you say?"

"I guess so, Edward. I could use a rest, too." Nicholas made his way to the strawberry patch. He ate some of the small, sweet berries. "Mmm. They taste like summertime," Nicholas said between mouthfuls. "We'll talk about moving on after a good meal and some rest."

Edward chose a cozy opening in the wall for his nap. The opening had a big flat stone on top and soft moss growing inside. He could look out at the world and still be safe. He felt like a prince surveying his kingdom. Edward fell asleep dreaming of a stone castle and brave knights.

Nicholas chose an opening closer to the ground that went deep into the wall. He stored some nuts in case he woke up hungry. He fell asleep dreaming he was flying. From way up in the sky, he could see how far they still had to go to reach the coast.

Chapter Eleven

The sun set later as summer came along and the weather grew warmer. Nicholas and Edward used the long days to explore. They made friends with a white-tail deer named Bobbin. Sometimes Bobbin carried them on her back as she bound through the trees.

"Watch out, low branch," Bobbin said, laughing. Nicholas and Edward, clinging to the fur on her back, lay down flat. Pine tassels tickled their backs. Bobbin loved to run among the trees and through the fields. "Hang on, we're almost to the top of the hill," she said, leaping over a stone wall.

"At least we're on the ground," Edward said. He still remembered his flight with Alfred.

"I hitched a ride with a sheep once," Nicholas said. "She never moved as fast as you." He looked up in time to see another pine branch. "Where are we going in such a hurry?"

"Isn't it exciting to run through the trees? No coyote or fox can keep up with me. Take a look at the view from up here," Bobbin said, slowing to a walk.

"This whole valley was once the home of four towns and many small villages," Bobbin said. They were standing on a hillside on the long peninsula dividing the lake. "Long ago, growing cities in the eastern part of the state needed more water. People there decided the deep valleys and many rivers of this area made an ideal location to build a reservoir. They bought all the houses and businesses here, built dams on the river, and flooded the whole valley."

"What happened to all the people?" Nicholas asked.

"Some stayed nearby to work on the dams and some moved away. Now this is a wonderful, wild place. I've raised all my fawns here," Bobbin said. "Some of the farms high up on the hillsides weren't covered with water. Over time, trees grew in the untended fields. Now the stone walls that surrounded those fields run through the forest."

"You can still see old roads," Nicholas said, looking down from the hill.

"Yes, there are old cellar openings in the woods

where houses used to stand. More than once I almost fell into one running through the trees."

After a lunch of early blackberries, the animals wandered down the hill to a low swampy area. Aspen trees grew close together, straight and tall. Red maples grew on patches of dry ground. Bog laurel and cattails surrounded the wet spots. Bobbin carefully picked her way through the soft ground. They heard someone muttering from within a thicket.

The voice said, "Now, I know it's around here somewhere. Say, that tree looks familiar for sure," it continued. The branches of a young locust tree parted and a beaver waddled out. "Prickly little trees, I must say. Hello there," the beaver paused when he saw Bobbin.

The beaver shook loose leaves that were clinging to his fur. "I'm in a bit of a tangle. I've lived around here all my life, but these days I get lost easily. I can't seem to find my den. Have you seen it? It's sort of mound-shaped with lots of twigs and mud?"

"We haven't passed one," Bobbin said, smiling. "But I did see what looked like the beginning of a beaver dam over near a stand of willow trees."

"Ah yes, that sounds about right. I started the new dam and den recently. It is to be something of a small retirement den. Everything will be on one level and very convenient. If I find the dam, I'm sure to find the den," the beaver chuckled. "You've been most kind." The beaver headed off in the wrong direction.

Bobbin bounded off after the beaver. "Not that way,

it's over this way," she said, heading toward the beaver's dam.

"Oh, dear me," the beaver said. "I'll never keep up with such a quick-moving deer."

"Maybe we can help," Nicholas said, hopping down to the ground.

"And who might you be, young fellow?" the startled beaver asked.

"I'm Nicholas, and this is my friend, Edward. We have been spending some time in this area, but really we are on our way to the coast."

"The coast, you say?" the beaver said. "I don't know as I've heard of any coast around here. My name is Maxwell. Mostly everyone calls me Max. So you think you can help me find my way?"

"I'm sure of it," Nicholas said. "What do you say, Edward? Should we stay around and help Max? We can go with him when he heads out for the day and guide him home afterward."

"That doesn't sound like hard work at all. It will give me plenty of time for naps and snacks during the day," Edward said.

"Good-bye for now, Nicholas and Edward," Bobbin said. "I will see you again." With that, the deer sprang off with a flash of her white tail.

Nicholas and Edward spent the rest of the summer with the beaver. Maxwell showed Nicholas a plan to build a bridge over the pond from his den to the shore. The project took them to the forest to collect branches and small trees. Nicholas and Maxwell were up early but took breaks often for snacks. Maxwell told many stories of his younger days on the reservoir. Nicholas followed along, keeping track of the way back to the den and listening to Maxwell's tales. Over the course of the summer, Nicholas learned a great deal about the unique area surrounding the Quabbin Reservoir.

Chapter Twelve

Edward enjoyed the slow pace of the summer. He had taken to writing poetry and sleeping late. He enjoyed a quiet breakfast and then wandered off to create his verse. His poetry featured his own adventures. "Now what rhymes with courageous, I wonder?" he said to himself one afternoon as he sat atop a stone wall.

"How about nervous?" someone replied from behind the wall.

"No, I was thinking more along the lines of tremendous," Edward said, looking around.

"Are you sure you don't want to say nervous?" a red fox asked. He placed his black forepaws up on the wall and prepared to leap.

"Now, let's not be hasty," Edward said, in a very nervous voice. "You don't want to jump up here after me. This wall is very wobbly. Maybe you can help me with my poem? Let me recite it for you."

The red fox was clever and patient, and he was hungry. He thought he could outsmart this tiny chipmunk. The fox wanted to be sure. "Alright, I will help you with your poem. Let me hear it."

Edward stood still with his chin held high and his chest puffed out.

A heroic animal fought his way,
through forest, field, and swamp,
to home and family, and hear them say,
"Hurray for Edward, our lost chipmunk"

He fought off a bobcat and soared with a goose,
with cunning, and a stout heart,
Edward, the courageous

"That's where I am stuck," Edward said. "I need a word to rhyme with courageous." He looked down at the fox.

"No, you are confused," the fox said, thinking. "You need to rhyme with heart, not courageous, to keep your rhyming pattern."

Edward went over the poem in his head. "You are right. Can you suggest a line for me?"

The fox did not want to be outsmarted by the chipmunk. He began to think. He closed his eyes. He mumbled a few words to himself. Edward saw his opportunity and ran off.

That evening Edward sat outside Max's den with Nicholas. The sun was setting earlier now. Edward recounted his adventure for them.

"You're lucky that fox didn't eat you up," Max said. "Even a clever chipmunk will run out of luck eventually."

"I knew what I was doing the whole time," Edward boasted. "Nicholas, you should have seen that silly old fox standing there with his eyes closed."

"I'm glad you're safe," Nicholas said. "But I think Max is right. You should be careful. Quabbin is a wild place."

Edward chuckled to himself, very pleased with his heroics.

"Max," Nicholas said. "You have never told me what the word Quabbin means?"

"The Nipmuck Indians, who lived in this part of the state, called it Qaben. The word means 'meeting of waters'," Maxwell explained. "Indians lived throughout the state of Massachusetts. Their names for places are a reminder of their long history with the land."

"This area has seen so much change, hasn't it?" Nicholas asked. "First the Indians lived here alone,

then Europeans came and made farms and towns. Now the land is protected as the Quabbin Reservoir."

"What are some other Indian names for things we might know?" Edward asked.

"Why, you are," Max said. "Not your name, Edward, but who you are. Chipmunk is an Indian word. So are skunk, moose, and raccoon. Even the state's name, Massachusetts, comes from an Indian tribe name."

"There is a mountain," Max continued, "to the east, called Wachusett. It means 'the great hill'."

"To the east of here, did you say?" Nicholas asked. Edward and Nicholas looked at each other. They had spent so much time at Quabbin. It was time to continue their journey.

"Edward, we need to be on our way."

"You are right, Nicholas," Edward said. "Summer is nearly past. We need to keep moving if we want to get to the coast before winter."

"It sounds like we should head for that mountain" Nicholas said. "We might be able to see the coast from the top."

"I know someone who lives on Wachusett Mountain who can help you," Max said. "She is a raccoon named Stella. She has lived on the mountain for many years. I am sure that Bobbin will give you a ride."

Nicholas and Edward went to sleep that night in their rock-wall home for the last time. The next day they would be off in search of the mountain that stands alone.

Chapter Thirteen

Bobbin bounded along in the early morning mist. Her fur was wet with dew. The air had a chill to it. The deer ran through orchards and fields as she made her way east. The fields sported short grass after haying season. The orchards smelled sweet with nearly ripe apples. As he rode along on her back, Nicholas wondered what his parents were doing at home.

Bobbin watched a distant mountain grow closer. It stood alone, rising up out of a forest of oak, pine, spruce, and maple trees. Wide grass trails snaked down one side of the mountain.

"I think I can get to the mountain before nightfall," Bobbin said. They had paused for a rest and some food next to a farm pond. "We have been making good progress all day," she added, grazing on some mushrooms growing in a low spot near the pond.

"How are we going to find Maxwell's friend the raccoon?" Nicholas asked as he and Edward shared some sunflower seeds they found in the field. Wachusett was the biggest mountain he had ever seen.

"Well," Edward said. "I tell you what. If Bobbin can get us to the mountain, I think I know how to find Stella."

"Edward, you're always full of surprises," Nicholas said. "I just hope we can find her. If we find her quickly, she can help us on our way. I'm sure my parents are worried about me."

"We'll find her alright, Nicholas," Edward said. "Or I should say, we will let her find us."

The trio carried on until dusk. The ground was rising up and Bobbin walked cautiously among stones and brush under a canopy of trees. A stream spilled over a tumble of rocks. The water collected in a pool surrounded by a stand of hemlock trees.

"It's late. I think I'll spend the night here," Bobbin said. "I can return to Quabbin early. Will you two be safe here?"

"It is lovely here," Nicholas said. "It was very kind of you to bring us so far."

The deer folded her legs beneath her body and fell right to sleep.

The next morning Nicholas woke up to find Bobbin had gone. Edward slept soundly nearby. It was another cool morning. Nicholas got up to explore the area. They were in a park visited often by people. He found some picnic tables in a little clearing near the running stream. A garbage barrel contained the remains of visitors' lunches. Two crows stood on the rim of the barrel poking at a soggy paper bag. A third crow, on the ground near the barrel, tore apart the remains of a peanut butter and jelly sandwich.

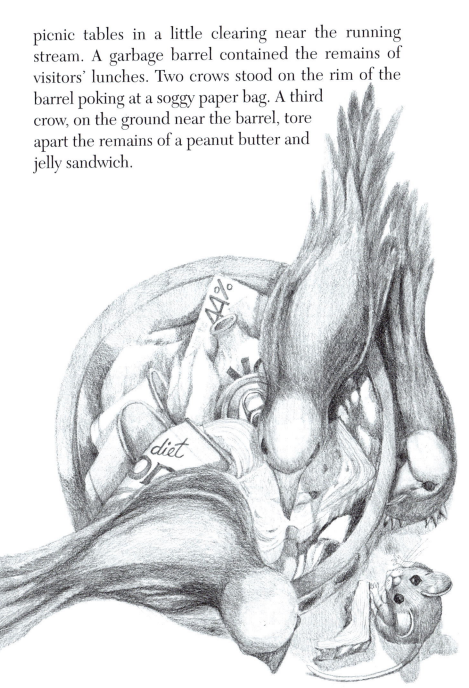

"Hello there, little fella," Rupert, the crow on the ground, said. "Are you looking for something to eat? There's always plenty of food after people have come to the park."

"I am hungry. Is there enough for my friend Edward, too?"

"Certainly there is. Calvin, toss down some more of that sandwich."

One of the crows on the barrel looked up. "You haven't finished what you have there."

"Now don't be greedy," Jeffery, the third crow, said. "There's plenty for all."

"I'm not being greedy, it's just that most of the garbage up here is soggy. That sandwich is the pick of the barrel."

Rupert fluttered up to the rim of the barrel. "Never mind, Calvin, I'll find something." Rupert poked his beak into a second sandwich bag.

"I'm just saying, it's always the same. I find a tasty sandwich and Rupert comes along and wants the best bits," Calvin said.

"That's not true. I shared half a watermelon I found the other day, didn't I?" Rupert said. "I didn't complain. I was more than happy to share what I found. Share and share alike, I always say."

While the other two birds continued to argue, Rupert tossed down the remains of the sandwich to Nicholas.

"Here you go, young fella. Bring that to your friend. There will be plenty left after these two are done," Rupert said.

Nicholas thanked the crow and skittered back to Edward, who was sipping water from the stream. Nicholas told Edward about the crows, the garbage barrel, and all the food scattered on the ground.

"Nicholas, I believe you have found the spot where we shall wait for Stella. I don't think she will come around until nightfall. Let's stay near this picnic area today and see what happens."

Chapter Fourteen

Nicholas watched visitors come and go all day. Many brought backpacks and spent the day hiking the mountain trails. Families stopped and ate at the picnic tables beside the stream. By the end of the day, all sorts of cast-off food filled the garbage barrel.

The smell of food drew Nicholas to the barrel again. Edward watched from the shadows of a hemlock tree. Nicholas nibbled at a bit of cookie on the ground. From there, he noticed crumbs under the table. He dashed from the barrel to the table.

An open backpack on the ground next to the table looked interesting. Nicholas climbed in. The bag was dark and warm inside. A small stuffed bear, resting on a folded wool sweater, surprised Nicholas. "Oh, hello there, Mr. Bear," Nicholas said. "I didn't know anyone was in here." The bear stared at Nicholas with his button eyes.

"We are looking for someone who lives around here. Her name is Stella. Do you know her?" The whole bag suddenly shifted and the bear leaned over. "You must be tired. I'll let you lay down," Nicholas said. "My friend Edward and I have been traveling for weeks. We're both headed for the coast."

Nicholas could hear his friend calling from outside the bag. "Do you mind if I climb onto your shoulders to see out?" Nicholas asked. He could hear Edward again. Gently as a mouse, Nicholas stood on Mr. Bear's back and peeped out of the flap. Nicholas saw the young boy had put his backpack on and was walking along a mountain trail with his family. Nicholas saw Edward on the picnic table jumping up and down.

Nicholas had to find a way to get the boy to stop. "I beg your pardon Mr. Bear, but I need your help. If I boost you up, will you get the boy to stop so that I can get out?" The bear didn't seem to object, so Nicholas pushed the stuffed bear up over his head. It was hard for Nicholas to get a grip on the slippery nylon bag, but he finally got Mr. Bear to the top.

The stuffed animal flipped over the edge of the bag and landed with a thump on the trail. The little boy turned around when he heard the sound. "Now how did you get out of my backpack, Mr. Bear?" The boy set his pack on the ground and dusted off his bear.

"Thank you, Mr. Bear," Nicholas shouted as he hopped out of the open bag. He ran for cover among some old red oak trees. The little boy set the bear back in his bag and ran to catch up with his family.

Edward found Nicholas under the trees. "There you are, Nicholas! I thought I was going to have to chase you all the way up the mountain. Come on. I think we should stay together for the rest of the day." The two animals made their way back to the stream and waited for dusk.

All the visitors were out of the park and the sun was setting. Nicholas and Edward had eaten their fill from the barrel. They sat on some stones near

the stream, waiting. From within the trees they heard a rustling and rumbling.

"My goodness, let's see what they left today. There's always more than I can eat, that is for sure. I'll have to wash off whatever I find. Dirt and dust on everything, I suspect." The biggest raccoon Nicholas had ever seen came waddling out of the woods.

"Well, who's this?" the raccoon said. "There's always somebody around the garbage barrel at the end of the day. If it isn't those pesky crows, it's some other animal."

Nicholas hopped up. "You must be Stella. My friend Edward and I have been waiting for you all day. Maxwell from over in the Quabbin sent us here to look for you."

"All day you say? I've been sleeping in my den most of the day. You know Maxwell, you say?"

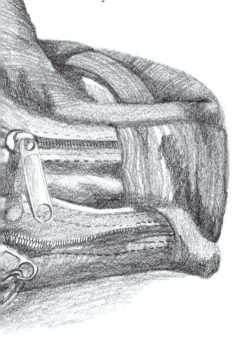

"We didn't know where to look for you, but Edward here had an idea how to find you," Nicholas said.

"You're the clever one, eh?" she said to Edward.

"You see, what I determined was that if we could find a source of food, we would surely find animals such as yourself," Edward said.

"Well, you found me. You can tell me what you're after while I pick out something for my supper."

Nicholas told Stella their story and how they needed her help.

"You want to find the coast, eh?" Stella carried her food to the stream. She took care, washing off a slice of cantaloupe from the garbage barrel. "I can tell you. Yes, I can. But, it sounds like others have told you how to find the coast." She bit into the fruit. "I'll tell you what. I'll show you the coast. You follow me. It's a hike for sure." Stella finished her meal and washed her paws in the stream. "Do you think you can climb this here mountain?"

Stella headed toward the woods. At the edge of the trees she stopped. "You mind where I go. You'll see the coast when we get to the top of the mountain."

Chapter Fifteen

Stella made her way up the mountain, over rocks and under fallen trees. Nicholas and Edward kept up with the bigger animal because Stella stopped often. She stopped to catch her breath and to rest. She stopped to admire the landscape. Sometimes she just stopped to talk.

"Sure enough, this land all belonged to native people long ago. They lived all through here. They even fought a war with the English here. Sad times, I am sure," Stella was saying. "Animals know the history. We remember and tell the stories from one generation to the next. Isn't that so?"

"My family's journal is how we remember the old times."

"You know, my family is one of the oldest back east," Edward said.

"Come on, it's best we keep moving," Stella said.

The three animals were approaching a part of the old forest. The going was slow. The ground was steep and rocky. The trees were large but grew bent over from years of strong winds and rain.

"These are the oldest trees around," Stella said, pointing to a red oak tree. "Long ago, loggers and farmers couldn't get to these last trees. I guess the ground was just too steep. So, the trees just grew and grew."

"Those trees have seen a lot of history, haven't they, Stella?" Nicholas said.

"That's right, my young friend. Some of the trees are 350 years old. Imagine that."

"They started growing right after the *Mayflower* arrived. They were young trees during the American Revolution, and now look—they're still going," Edward said.

"I like to think of all the people and animals that have passed through history," Stella said. "People are history, not just wars and such. People and their stories."

"Don't forget the animals, too. We play our part in history." Stella wiped her face with her paws. "All kinds of animals—cows, horses, and even pigs—play a part in history," Stella said. "'Course, not just them. Beavers, birds, you name it, they had a hand in history."

The sun had set long ago. They left

the oak trees behind. It was dark and cold. Stars peeked through the leaves from above. They trudged on silently. The trees thinned out and the ground leveled off. It felt mostly stony and cold to Nicholas. Stella was ahead sniffing the night air.

"We'll wait here. It won't take long," she said sitting down. "You two stay close. Old Stella will keep you warm." The two small animals moved in next to Stella, enjoying the warmth of her soft fur.

Nicholas must have dozed off. He was dreaming his mom was welcoming him home, safe and sound, with a big hug. However, the voice he heard wasn't his mom's and he felt a nudge.

"Now pay attention and look off that way." Stella gestured with her head toward the horizon.

The sky was clear, pale blue. Thin strips of jagged clouds streaked the horizon. They were black on top and washed with bright orange on the bottom. All at once, the sun emerged. The whole world seemed to be waking up. Birds called from the trees. Nicholas cheered and Stella said, "That's right. That's the best show around. She never disappoints. Now wait 'til the sun climbs a bit."

"I don't believe I have ever seen such a sunrise," Edward said.

"I reckon that's true," Stella said. "You're standing on the highest land for a long ways around."

The sun rose higher. It lit up the land in a golden path from the sea to the base of the mountain.

"Now, look east as far as you can. That sparkle you see, way out there, is the ocean. That's the coast."

Nicholas was speechless. That was his destination. He never realized what he had gotten into. He was just a little mouse. Even with Edward's help, how was he going to get all the way to the coast? And, if he made it to the coast, how would he find his uncle?

Stella must have been reading his mind. "Now, don't you worry, Nicholas. I know it looks a long way off.

I wouldn't have shown you the coast if I didn't have a way of getting you there. We'll have to hurry, though. We can't spend our time daydreaming up here. Now hurry and follow me."

Stella headed down the other side of the mountain. Nicholas wondered how she was going to get them to the coast. Edward shrugged, followed along behind, and wondered why they always had to hurry everywhere.

Chapter Sixteen

Stella led the way down the mountain. Sometimes, she tumbled head over heels on the steep parts. Nicholas and Edward found a path among the boulders and tree roots. They came to the grassy trails used by skiers in the winter and they stopped on a granite ledge.

"In the winter I don't venture too far from my den. But sometimes I am out and about on a clear day and, I tell you, I've seen some strange things on these trails." Nicholas looked down the slope.

"See those poles with chairs?" Stella asked. "Well, I've seen folks ride them to the top of the mountain. They strap boards to their feet and slide this way and that on the snow. As soon as they get to the bottom, they ride the chair back up and do it all over again. It just makes no sense," Stella said, shaking her head.

"What's in that building?" Nicholas asked, looking at the base of the mountain.

"That's where we are headed," Stella said. "If we get down there in time, that is."

Stella headed off again. When they reached the base of the mountain, Stella hid under a big deck built on the back of the building. "Now we just wait here," she said to Nicholas and Edward, who crouched next to her.

"What exactly are we waiting for?" Edward asked. "We certainly got here in a hurry."

"Why, we're waiting for your ride to the coast," Stella said. "A truck from a big city on the coast stops here every week in the fall."

"A truck?" Nicholas asked. "How will we ever get on a truck?"

"Be patient. I'll show you how when that truck gets here," Stella said. They didn't have long to wait. A yellow-and-blue truck rolled up to the building.

"I told you it would come. That truck is full of seafood. Now they're going to have to unload the fish. When they go in the building, that's your chance. Now, stay out of sight."

Two men from the truck opened the back and walked into the building with big plastic totes. Nicholas could see mist roll out of the truck.

"It looks kind of cold in there," he said.

"Well, I suspect so. They want to keep the fish fresh now, don't they?" Stella said. "It won't be cold on the way back when the truck is empty now, will it?" she added.

Nicholas had his doubts, but he had to trust Stella. He didn't see any other way.

"Now's our chance," Stella said. "We best make a run for it."

Nicholas and Edward ran along behind. They got to the big open doors and stared up. Stella stretched up, put her front paws on the truck, and called over her shoulder, "Climb on up, fellas. I'll hold on while you get inside."

Nicholas and Edward scrambled over Stella's back and jumped from her head. They turned around to face her from inside the truck. "Good-bye, Stella. I'll never forget that sunrise."

"Yes, Stella, you have been more than kind," Edward added. "I shall always think kindly of you."

"Go on inside now," Stella said. "You don't want those two men to see you. I'll be waiting for word of you from my friends out in the wide world."

The door of the building opened. "There's no fish in there for you," Stella heard one of the men say. "Now scat." Stella hopped down and waddled off toward the trees. Nicholas and Edward hid under some burlap bags.

"Make sure there aren't any more raccoons up there," one man said to the other.

"Ah, it looks all clear," the other man said, closing the doors. "Let's get going. It looks like we're in for some weather. I don't like driving in the rain." The truck rumbled off with Nicholas and Edward bouncing around in the back.

There was no way to look outside. They could hear rain drumming on the roof and water splashing against the side of the truck. Edward kept up a running story about his family history. Mostly Nicholas dozed, dreaming he was riding on Shirley's back, headed home to his mom and dad.

Nicholas was jolted awake by the sound of squealing tires, then silence. The rain continued outside. As the door opened, a rumble of thunder boomed in the night. One man climbed up into the truck. Nicholas and Edward stayed hidden. "Grab those bags," the other man said. "When they're filled we can get them back."

They dropped the bags on the ground next to a metal building. Nicholas listened and heard the truck drive away. "Hey, Edward," he whispered. "Are you alright?" A flash of lightning lit up the night. Nicholas saw a house bobbing up and down in the storm. "Come on, Edward. Let's get inside."

The two small animals scrambled over ropes and nets and found a small opening in the side of the house. They curled up in a warm, snug spot. It was quiet and dry. As Nicholas fell asleep, he wondered about this unusual house and the adventures that lay ahead.

Chapter Seventeen

Nicholas opened his eyes to a world in motion. He looked out from under a table attached to the wall. Raincoats on hooks, a towel hanging from the stove, and a basket of fruit suspended from the ceiling swung back and forth.

Edward awoke nearby. "I don't think I feel so good," he groaned.

"Good morning, Edward," Nicholas said cheerfully. Sparkling sunlight filled the small room. "It isn't raining anymore, but this little house is jumping all over the place." Nicholas tried his feet on the moving floor. "I think I can get up to the window. Maybe I can see what's going on."

"See if you can make it stop moving," Edward said, rolling over and shutting his eyes.

Nicholas scampered up to the window ledge. "Edward, there is water all around! We're on a boat. Isn't this fun?"

"No, it's not fun. My stomach is moving around too much for this to be fun."

"I have never seen such a sight in all my life," Nicholas said. He heard scratching at the door. A black snout nosed it open. A Labrador puppy bounded in. He sniffed around, zeroing in on Edward. The pup barked sharply, twice.

"Oh, go away," Edward groaned. "I'm in no mood to play."

"What are you doing on my boat?" the puppy asked. He sniffed at Edward. The dog's wet nose was close enough for Edward to feel his puppy breath. The dog's tail wagged happily in the air.

"If I had known how a boat rolls, I would never have come," Edward said, opening one eye. "You can believe that."

"Isn't it the best?" the dog asked. "This is my third trip and I still love it." The puppy bounded over to the stove and shook the towel hanging there in a playful sort of way. The towel pulled free and the dog sat back with a bump. He looked up and saw Nicholas.

"Hey there, little mouse. What are you doing here? Did you sign on to go fishing, too?"

"We just wanted to get out of the storm last night.

Where are we going?"

"We're headed for the greatest fishing spot in the world," the puppy said. "Fishing boats have been sailing out of Gloucester for years, headed for the Grand Banks. When we get back I can show you around."

"Will we be back tonight?" Nicholas asked.

"Tonight? No, we'll still be steaming out to the fishing grounds tonight. We could be gone for a week or more. It all depends on the fishing. Isn't that awesome?"

"A week," Edward sat up. His eyes were bloodshot and the fur on his head stood out in all directions. "I don't think I will live that long."

"Ah, you'll be alright," the puppy said. "My dad said he always got sick the first day at sea, but he got used to the motion." The information didn't cheer up Edward any. He fell over in a heap.

"Is your dad on the boat, too?" Nicholas asked.

"No, he's back home. He says he's too old to go fishing anymore. My dad taught me all about fishing. The captain lets me come now. Do you want to come out on deck? I can show you around."

"Sure. What do you think, Edward? Do you want to see the boat?" Edward lifted his arm and weakly waved them on.

"My name is Antonio, but my dad calls me Tony. What's your name?"

"I'm Nicholas, sometimes my mom calls me Nick."

"It's nice to meet you, Nick. You have to be careful out here. As my dad always says, there are more ways to get hurt on a fishing boat than almost anywhere else."

The two animals were out on the stern deck of the red-and-white deep-sea trawler. "Doesn't the sea air smell great?" Tony said. He darted around the ropes and cables. He shivered in his excitement. "Come on," he said, disappearing behind the big cable winch.

"When we haul the net back up on deck, it will be full of wiggling fish. The crew sorts them out and stores the fish in the hold."

"What's your job?" Nicholas asked.

"My job is to keep the captain company when he's running the boat. The crew will be on deck. I stay with him mostly. Actually," Tony said, looking toward the wheelhouse, "I am supposed to be up there right now. You should check on your seasick friend." He headed forward, taking the roll of the fishing boat in stride.

Nicholas stayed on deck by himself. He breathed in the clean, cold salt air. The boat charged on, heading out to sea. Land fell farther and farther astern as the boat rode up and over each wave. He had made it to the coast at last, he thought. And yet, Nicholas felt no closer to finding his uncle now than when he started out months before.

Chapter Eighteen

Days passed. Edward recovered enough to get up and look around a bit. The crew worked day and night catching fish. They worked in fair weather and foul. Nicholas learned everything he could about fishing from Tony.

"My dad says fishermen from many countries have come to these fishing grounds for hundreds of years," Tony told Nicholas. "They sailed their ships across the Atlantic Ocean looking for fish to feed people back home."

"The fishermen set up fishing stations all over New England. My home port, Gloucester, is the most famous one of all. There's a big bronze statue of a fisherman right on the waterfront in town," Tony said. He and Nicholas were down below. Tony was eating his dinner and Nicholas was nibbling a piece of biscuit left over from the crew's meal. The crew was up on deck hauling in the last load of fish for the day.

"There weren't always big motorboats to fish from," Tony continued. "Long ago, men built schooners with tall masts to sail to the fishing grounds. When the schooner reached the Grand Banks, the fishermen had to row out in small dories to catch fish. They came to know every section of water along the New England coast."

"Do you think they would know where West Tisbury is?" Nicholas asked. "I've come all the way from the western edge of Massachusetts looking for West Tisbury."

"I bet they would," Tony said. "You know who else might know? A gannet, a seabird friend of mine named Gilbert. Sometimes, we'll have a talk when we cross paths at sea. He knows the whole east coast."

"Will you see your friend on this trip?" Nicholas asked.

"You never can tell with seabirds," Tony said. "Sometimes they fly in close to the boat, sometimes they keep their distance. Come on. Let's see if we can find Gilbert."

The two went out on deck again. The crew was finishing their day's work. They were too busy to pay any attention to Tony and Nicholas. It was getting late and the sun was setting. As the bright orange ball dipped below the horizon, it filled the sky with a light and color Nicholas had never seen on land.

In the gathering dusk, Nicholas noticed four or five birds skimming over the wave tops. As they drew closer, Nicholas watched one bird rise up, hover over the water, then dive, folding his sharp wings as he plunge down into the sea.

"There he is!" Tony shouted. "Over here, Gilbert. Gilbert, it's me." Tony jumped up and down, yipping and yapping. The graceful seabird dipped one wing and carved a turn in the air, heading toward the trawler.

"Good to see you, Tony," Gilbert said, hovering behind the boat. "How's the fishing?"

"Well, the boat is nearly full. The captain says soon we'll head for shore to sell our catch."

"That's a good idea. As I flew high in the sky, I saw a big storm headed this way. I don't think you want to be out on the ocean during that storm," Gilbert said.

"Gilbert, this is my friend Nicholas," Tony said, pointing his nose at the mouse. "He sort of stowed away on the boat when we left Gloucester."

"Is that so?" Gilbert asked, swooping in close to look at Nicholas. "Why did you want to go to sea? It's a dangerous place for such a young mouse."

"We didn't exactly want to go to sea," Nicholas said. "My friend Edward and I have been traveling for months. I'm looking for a town called West Tisbury. Have you heard of it?" Nicholas asked.

"West Tisbury?" Gilbert asked.

"That's right," Nicholas said. "It's very important. My parents are counting on me. I have to find my uncle who lives there."

"I know the place," Gilbert said. "It's on an island to the south of here. It's on the other side of Cape Cod, south of Boston."

"We're headed to Boston with this load of fish," Tony said. "I bet you can find it when we get there."

"Remember," Gilbert said as he flew away. "You should head for land as soon as you can." He was just a small speck now in the darkening sky.

Nicholas was happy. He knew he was getting closer to his destination, even though he was still miles out to sea. And, there was an ocean storm out there somewhere.

Chapter Nineteen

All night the waves grew bigger. The motion of the boat became rougher. The crew went out on deck and secured everything they could. Tony stayed with the captain in the wheelhouse watching angry green waves wash over the bow. Nicholas and Edward huddled together under the table.

The trawler rumbled along. It climbed up the back of the great waves. The boat paused briefly and then slid down the front until the bow plowed into the next wave. Huge sheets of spray flew out from each side of the boat. The boat struggled up the next wave, repeating the wild ride.

The rolling motion threw everything loose onto the deck. Empty pots, dishes, forks, and spoons slid around where Nicholas and Edward lay. It all skidded back and forth in a tangled, wet mess. The two animals were about as miserable as they could be. Nicholas watched water pool on the deck. It covered more and more space as time went by.

"I can't believe what's happening. Everything seemed fine just a few hours ago. Now it's all just one big soggy heap," Edward said. He shook his head in disbelief.

"This reminds me of the flood back home," Nicholas said. "Does it look like the water is rising in here?"

"I believe it is. What happens if it keeps going up? Will we sink?"

The water level continued to rise. Nicholas and Edward scrambled up to the tabletop. They slid around on the slick surface.

"Nicholas, I think you better get Tony down here. He can call for help. We are definitely sinking."

Nicholas fought off his fear and leapt for a mug floating by. He paddled his way to the stairs. The stairs led to the wheelhouse. He could see the captain standing

at the wheel trying to keep the boat on course. Tony lay curled up on the captain's bunk. Nicholas squeaked loudly so that Tony could hear him over the storm. Tony lifted his head and looked down at Nicholas.

"Nicholas, what are you doing up here? It's not safe for you to be moving about in this storm."

"You've got to come with me, Tony. The boat is filling up with water. I think we're sinking," Nicholas said. Tony jumped from the bunk and followed Nicholas down below.

"I think we can turn on the pumps, but I will need your help. There is a switch on the wall that is too high for me to reach," Tony said. "Nicholas, you and Edward climb on my back." The two wet animals clung to Tony as he swam through the water over to the wall.

"Do you see that red button up there?" he asked Nicholas. "That will turn the pump on and get rid of the water in the boat." Tony stretched up as high as he could. Edward scurried up and stood on the puppy's head. Nicholas followed and stood on Edward's shoulders. He could just reach the switch. With all his might, he pushed on the red button. They heard a whirring sound that meant the pump had started. Slowly the water began to recede.

Nicholas and Edward watched the cabin dry out. The captain came below and saw the mess. He picked up Tony and wrapped him in a towel. "There you are, you little rascal. I let one of the crew steer the boat when I noticed you were gone from the wheelhouse."

Tony licked the captain's face. "Look's like we have a lot of cleaning up to do in here," the captain said, "but I think the storm is winding down."

Nicholas and Edward watched from the back of the shelf. They were glad the storm was passing. They wanted to get back to dry land and get off the boat.

By morning, the storm was over. The trawler was making its way toward Boston Harbor. They passed a lighthouse on Little Brewster Island.

"That's the oldest lighthouse in America," Tony said. Nicholas and Edward were looking out the galley window at the sights.

"Soon, the city of Boston will come into view," Tony said. "We're headed for the fish pier. Boston is such a big city; you're sure to find someone there who will help you get to West Tisbury."

Nicholas watched the buildings grow larger as they approached the city. Even Edward was quiet, trying to take in all the sights. Big jet airplanes landed at the airport nearby. Small boats and big ships went about their business in the harbor. The trawler slowed and landed with a gentle bump at the pier. They had arrived in the state capital.

Neither Nicholas nor Edward knew where to turn next. They looked out at the hustle and bustle of the city and realized their adventure was about to change.

Chapter Twenty

Nicholas watched all the activity from the window. Workers laughed and argued as they unloaded the catch. Seagulls screamed overhead. Cranes whirred, lifting fish from the boats. Trucks zoomed onto the pier. Buyers haggled over prices. Fish, packed in ice, left the pier headed to markets all over the state.

Edward joined him. "Now this is more like it. The boat has stopped moving. We are back on land and getting closer to my home all the time."

"Tony said we should hitch a ride on the crane lifting fish off of our boat," Nicholas said. "We can hide in the totes full of fish."

Nicholas and Edward tried to stay out of the way of the fast-moving crew. Everyone was eager to finish unloading and head back to Gloucester.

Nicholas watched the crew stack totes on the deck. The crane picked them up and set them on the pier where other men weighed them on a scale. Seagulls perched everywhere watching for anything that would make a meal. The two animals crept closer to the action.

"If we time our jump just right, we can get on one of those totes without the crew seeing us," Nicholas said.

"I don't want to spend any more time with those fish," Edward said. "Isn't there another way off this boat?"

"Come on, Edward, this might be our only chance." With that, Nicholas made a leap for the tote, scrambling in just as one of the crew put another tote on top. Nicholas looked out from the space between them. "Hurry up, Edward. We don't want to get separated now."

Edward jumped on top of the last tote just as the crane lifted them off the boat.

"Hey, where did you come from, little guy?" one of the crew said. "I didn't know we had a stowaway."

Everyone laughed watching Edward rise in the air and land with a bump on the pier. The seagulls swooped in and pecked at Edward.

"You watch that now," Edward said to the gull. "I'm not some fish bait for your meal." All the gulls were in the air now in a flurry of white feathers.

"Come on, Edward," Nicholas said, hopping from his tote. "Let's get out of here." He shoved Edward forward as he swatted away the gulls. They both ran toward the land.

The fishermen watching the scene laughed at the retreating animals. "I guess that chipmunk doesn't want to become a fisherman like us," one said as they all went back to work.

Nicholas and Edward dodged people, trucks, and the pesky seagulls as they ran off the pier and down the street. They followed people streaming along the sidewalk. A small building with a large T-sign ahead seemed to be their destination. A determined seagull made one last dive at Edward as he and Nicholas entered the glass door.

"We'll be safe from the birds in here," Nicholas said. They bounded down the steps. The people hurrying by paid no attention to the small animals. Everyone arrived in an underground room and stopped at the edge of a road.

Nicholas noticed another mouse sniffing around the

edge of the room. He went over to talk. "Hello there, can you help my friend and me? I'm Nicholas. What's your name?"

"I'm Patrick. What do you two want?"

"We're trying to find our way south, can you direct us?"

"Yeah, I can help ya. You see, what you want to do is take this Silver Line bus heya," he pointed to the empty roadway. "Get off at South Station. Take the Red Line in to Park Street. From there, you can get to anywhere in the city you want to go." Patrick scurried off on business of his own.

Nicholas looked at Edward. "I didn't understand anything Patrick just said."

"Just follow me," Edward said as a big Silver Line double bus rolled up. "And don't get stepped on."

Nicholas avoided the feet of people moving forward. Everyone seemed to be intent on finding room on the crowded bus. Edward hopped up and Nicholas followed him. The doors swung closed. Silently, the bus headed into the tunnel. Nicholas could only see concrete—on the ground, on the walls, and overhead.

Nicholas slumped down on the floor of the bus. He was sad, tired, and lonely. He wanted to find his uncle but this bus was going down into a dark tunnel. He wondered where this bus would take them. Nicholas wondered how they would find their way back to the sunlight.

Chapter Twenty-One

The bus droned on in the dark. All at once, it came out into another big room, full of light and noise. They had arrived at South Station. People rushed here and there, never looking at each other.

A sign with an arrow pointing read, "Red Line." "Keep up, Nicholas. We want to make our connection," Edward said, heading for the stairs.

Nicholas caught up with him as a gray train screeched to a halt. People moved onto the train, Nicholas and Edward among them. Everyone lurched backward as the train took off.

"Park Street is next. Change there for the Green Line," Nicholas heard a voice from a speaker say after a few minutes.

"This is it, Nicholas. This is our stop," Edward said. They hurried around a corner, climbed some stairs, and finally emerged into the sunshine.

The view was as strange to Nicholas as the cold empty ocean. Tall buildings rose up all around them. Cars and taxis, buses, and bicycles crowded the streets. People of all shapes and sizes hurried this way and that. Someone was selling hot peanuts from a cart.

"You look lost, my young friend." A red squirrel stood in front of Nicholas. "I've seen that look before," the squirrel said. "You're from out of town, aren't you?"

"Yes, my friend and I are traveling together." Nicholas pointed at Edward, who was over at the peanut cart sniffing around.

"Well, you've got to be careful in the big city," the squirrel said. "I'll help you find your way around. This park is the Boston Common. I live across the river in

Cambridge. I teach young squirrels the history of the city. We come to Boston all the time." A group of young girls, all dressed alike, trooped by. The squirrel watched the group for a few minutes.

"What's your name?"

"Nicholas. What's yours?"

"Oliver. Wait here, Nicholas. I'll be right back." With that, the squirrel hopped off toward the peanut cart. The group of girls had Edward surrounded.

"Oh, he is so cute. Come here, little chipmunk. Do you want a peanut? Come here, I won't hurt you." The girls lured Edward one way and then another. Oliver leaped into a maple tree and trilled his best squirrel call.

"Oh, look at the little red squirrel. Come here, little squirrel. Oh, I want to take him home," a girl said as the group ran over to the tree. Edward made a dash for it.

The squirrel leaped from tree to tree, leading the girls down the path away from Edward. Oliver made his way back after losing the girls in the public garden.

"That was most kind of you," Edward said. "However, I was about to make a break when you arrived."

"Don't mention it," Oliver said. "Come with me. Let me show you the city."

All the trees were ablaze with the colors of fall. A golden dome atop a building on a hill shone through the branches.

"That building is the state capitol. It was built right after the American Revolution. Come on, let me show you the public garden." He crossed a street when the traffic stopped at a red light.

"I like to come to the garden in the spring when all the flowers are in bloom," Oliver told them. Nicholas stopped.

"Edward," Nicholas shouted. "Take a look at that swan. It's the biggest bird I've ever seen."

"That is a swan boat," Oliver said. "It's not a real swan. The plastic swan hides some pedals a person uses to move the boat through the water. Would you like to go for a boat ride? It is very peaceful floating along under the willow trees."

"I have had my fill of boats," Edward said. "Besides, we need to keep traveling south."

"Oliver, we're headed for West Tisbury," Nicholas said, explaining his journey to the red squirrel.

"I know just what you need to do. We need to get to the train station."

"Train station? We just came up from the subway," Nicholas said, following Oliver out of the park.

"Not that train. You'll see when we get there. It's on the other side of the city. I bet you haven't eaten yet today. Am I right?"

"I didn't even get a peanut before those girls took after me," Edward said.

"Well, follow me," Oliver said. "I know somewhere we can get all the food we want. And, it's on the way to the train."

Edward was more than happy to follow. Nicholas sighed. It seemed to him that his journey would never end. He had no choice now but to follow the red squirrel and hope he would guide them out of the city.

Chapter Twenty-Two

Nicholas and Edward followed Oliver back through the common. They dodged people walking their dogs, tourists following the Freedom Trail, and children playing baseball in the park. Oliver moved at the pace of a city dweller. Nicholas and Edward skipped along, trying to keep up with him. They stopped at a circle of cobblestones pressed into the road.

"That circle marks the sight of a battle during the Revolution," Oliver said. "You can travel down almost any street in the city and learn something about history."

"I have a friend who said history is stories about people, not just wars and big things," Nicholas said. "She says each one of us, no matter how small, plays a part in history."

"It's always the big folks who get talked about in history, isn't it?" Oliver said.

"I don't know what my part in history is going to be," Nicholas said.

"That's the thing of it, Nicholas, you can never tell how you will fit into history."

"My family goes quite far back in history," Edward said. "They have been around for centuries. Oh, the stories I could tell you."

"I'm sure you have quite a history," Oliver said. The three animals walked downhill toward a cluster of buildings. Everyone was busy. Shoppers wandered in and out of stores. People ate food as they walked. Flocks of pigeons ruffled around the rough stone sidewalks looking for lunch.

"They sell every kind of food here in Quincy Market," Oliver said. "We'll have no trouble finding some tasty tidbits here." They paused under a tree growing near the market. An old man addressed some tourists.

"Good day to you, kind folk," the man said, bowing low. "Welcome to our fair city." Nicholas watched the man from the shadows of a tree root.

"That man is pretending to be Benjamin Franklin," Oliver said. "He walks around the city talking to people about our country's history."

"People don't mind that?" Nicholas asked.

"No, I think people like to pretend along with him," Oliver said.

"You see, I was born in this city," Franklin was saying to the tourists. "I spent my youth here. My father wanted me to apprentice with him as a candle and soap maker, but I had other ideas."

"I have seen Philadelphia, London, and Paris, but I hold a special place for Boston. Ordinary people like Paul Revere and Abigail Adams made a difference in our history," Franklin went on. "Why, even our animals are interested in history," he said, pointing to Nicholas, Edward, and Oliver. They backed away into the shadows under the tree.

The crowd laughed. A boy holding a bag of popcorn in one hand and wearing a tricornered hat crouched down. He spread a few kernels of popped corn on the ground. Edward sniffed from a distance. His stomach rumbled. He shuffled his feet. He twitched his tail. He couldn't help himself. Edward grabbed some popcorn. He stuffed his cheeks as fast as he could.

Whomp went the hat, right over Edward. A little girl let go of her balloon in surprise and began to cry. Ben Franklin said, "Now see here, young man." The boy's mother tugged at the boy's shirt. The pigeons lifted up in a cloud of feathers and raced away. The boy fell over, pulling his hat off Edward. Nicholas scurried over the boy, grabbed Edward, and followed Oliver down the sidewalk away from the marketplace.

As they left the noise behind, Ben Franklin said, "Those animals have started a bit of a revolution of their own."

"Come on," Oliver said. "Let's go to the Haymarket. It's not so crowded and there's plenty of fresh food for lunch."

At the outdoor farmer's market, they found all sorts of fresh vegetables. Everyone was busy buying or selling. Nicholas had bits of an apple. Edward ate some string beans. Oliver nibbled corn on the cob.

"It is certainly nice to feel full again," Edward said. He leaned back against a sack of potatoes. "This meal reminds me of Thanksgiving back home. I always eat too much. You know, Nicholas, I really should be getting home. Oliver, how far is it to the train?"

"Not far. If you walk along the waterfront, you will be at the train station in no time. Look for the brick building with a big clock and a stone eagle on top. I have to get back to Cambridge. I have to teach my class soon. The young squirrels won't wait long if I'm not there on time. A train will be leaving the station this afternoon that will take you to Plymouth," Oliver said. "That's as far south as the trains run. From Plymouth, you will have to find your own way to West Tisbury."

Oliver called over his shoulder as he ran back along the waterfront, "Take care of each other, and watch out for the train conductors."

Nicholas and Edward set off, passing the Aquarium, the Children's Museum, and a fancy hotel. At last, they approached a big building with a clock on the outside.

"Ah yes, the Old Colony," Edward said. "That is my home. I'm afraid you will have to go on without me from there. Nicholas, you can find West Tisbury on your own, I am sure of it."

Nicholas had forgotten that Edward would leave him some day. He had grown to like the chipmunk and felt sad that they wouldn't always travel together. "You will come with me to Plymouth, won't you, Edward? Maybe you can help me find a way to travel south after Plymouth."

"Of course I will." Edward sniffled a little. "I always liked going to Plymouth at Thanksgiving time." He had grown fond of Nicholas, too. "Now let's find that train."

Chapter Twenty-Three

Nicholas and Edward had become old hands at getting on trains. They hid under a bench and watched the activity in the station. Above them, letters on a big black sign flipped over showing when trains were leaving. Passengers jumped off trains and headed into the city. People arrived at the station, wheeling luggage behind them. A loudspeaker made announcements.

Soon the loudspeaker blared out, "Old Colony Line, south to Plymouth, now loading track 12."

"That's us," Nicholas said. "Come on, Edward."

They scurried into the line of people headed for the train. They could see a tall skinny man with a blue uniform and a round hat helping people onto the train. "That must be the conductor," Edward said. "Follow me, Nicholas." The two animals hid behind a young woman pulling her luggage on wheels. She stopped to ask the conductor a question. Nicholas and Edward paused with her.

"Yes, miss, this is the train to Plymouth." The conductor looked down at the luggage. "Let me help you with your bag," he said, picking it up. Nicholas and Edward tried to hide behind the girl's shoe.

"Hey, wait a minute," the conductor said, seeing the animals. "You two can't ride the train."

Nicholas and Edward took off down the platform. The train whistle blew. "Last call for the Plymouth train," the speaker announced.

The conductor dodged among the boarding passengers, following Nicholas and Edward. "You two come back here. I can't let you on my train!"

He bumped into a passenger. He knocked a bag out of her hand, spilling its contents on the platform. He stopped to apologize and pick up the mess.

Seeing a chance to flee, Nicholas and Edward looked for an open door onto the train. The whistle blew again. The train started moving. As they ran, the train picked up speed. Nichols finally spied an open door.

"Quickly, Edward," he hollered. Nicholas leaped, Edward leaped, and the door began to close behind them. The conductor jumped aboard and the doors slid shut. The whistle blew again and the train left the station headed south.

The train clattered down the tracks through South

Shore towns. It stopped to let people off and to pick people up. Nicholas and Edward hid under a seat and kept an eye out for the conductor. He came through the car, collected tickets, and poked holes in them with a silver tool to mark the tickets as used. Little bits of paper sifted down to where Nicholas and Edward hid. The shreds of paper tickled Nicholas's nose. He held back as long as he could. Suddenly, he sneezed so hard that he tumbled out into the aisle—right next to the conductor's shoe.

"There you are!" he shouted. "I knew I would find you."

Nicholas ran down the aisle as the train rocked down the tracks. The conductor chased Nicholas from one car to the next. Edward puffed along behind them. Nicholas was at the end of the last car when the train screeched to a halt.

"Ah ha," the conductor said. "I've got you trapped at last!" Suddenly, the door opened and a loudspeaker announced, "Last stop, Plymouth. Everyone off here, please."

Nicholas jumped from the train. Edward ran between the conductor's legs and landed on the ground next to Nicholas. They took off into the bushes and trees at the end of the tracks. The conductor stood on the train with his hands on his hips and a puzzled look on his face.

Nicholas and Edward scurried through the bushes on a path that led to the ocean. They came to the

harbor. It was late afternoon on a gray November day. They were both tired and hungry. They wanted to find some food and shelter for the night.

"There it is," Edward said. He was pointing at a wooden ship floating next to a pier. It had tall masts and a maze of rigging. It was getting dark and fog flowed in from the sea.

"What is that?" Nicholas asked, looking up at the ship.

"Why, that's the old reproduction ship, *Mayflower II*," Edward said. "She's been floating in this harbor for years and years."

"I don't like the looks of it," Nicholas said. "There's something very strange about this ship."

"No one seems to be around. I bet we can find some food and someplace to sleep," Edward said.

"What if it takes off like that fishing boat in Gloucester? Remember, Edward?" Nicholas said.

Edward said, "Come on. Let's climb aboard." Edward marched up the gangway.

They couldn't make out much in the dark and fog. Nicholas heard the ship creak and groan softly as it rocked in the water. He wasn't so sure it was a good idea but he followed Edward onto the old wooden ship.

Chapter Twenty-Four

Nicholas and Edward padded onto the ship. The damp air smelled of tar. Nicholas looked up. The tall masts reminded him of pine trees in the forest back home. The black lines, running from mast to mast, looked like a spider's web.

Edward explored a cabin near the stern. He heard a squeak of surprise come from Nicholas toward the front of the ship. Edward ran forward searching for his friend. He found Nicholas face-to-face with a mink. Both animals tugged on a bit of salted fish.

"It's mine!" the mink said. "Let go."

Nicholas tugged back. "It was lying here on the deck. I found it."

"I've been collecting food on this ship for years. This is mine," the mink said. The two animals spun around each other holding the food.

"Now, now," Edward said, trying to calm them. "I'm sure there's enough for everyone."

They each pulled hard. The piece of fish tore in two, sending both animals rolling backward. Nicholas knocked over Edward, who spilled a bowl of oats.

"Ah, there you are now. Everyone has a bit of food and no harm done," Edward said, sitting up rubbing his head. He scooped up some oats and stored them in his cheeks.

Nicholas nibbled on the salt fish. The mink scurried onto a wooden chest. He took a bite out of his piece of fish. Feeling better now, he said, "What brings you two aboard *Mayflower II*?"

Nicholas and Edward looked at each other. "It's a long story," Edward said. "Right now we need a place to spend the night."

"Well, I'm Martin. I watch out for this old ship. You can stay aboard but you will have to be off by morning," the mink added. "The crew will come back, and then visitors will start showing up. They come to see the Pilgrims and hear their stories."

"Are there still Pilgrims on this ship?" Nicholas asked, looking around.

"No, this ship is a replica of the *Mayflower* that came here in 1620," Martin said. "The crew dress as Pilgrims and tell visitors what it was like to cross the ocean long ago."

"I grew up hearing about the Pilgrims," Edward said. "In fact, I've been told some of my family came over on the original *Mayflower*."

"I don't know about chipmunks," Martin said, "but I do know there were 102 passengers crowded together. Thirty-two of them were children. Everyone spent most of their time below deck, in the dark, for over two months."

"Did any animals come with them?" Nicholas asked.

"They had some goats, pigs, and chickens. Someone brought two dogs." Martin lowered his voice and said, "And, they say, all ships back then had cats. If you pardon my saying so, the cats were there to keep the rats and mice in check."

"I bet my dad would find a way around those cats,"

Nicholas said. "My dad," Nicholas repeated, remembering his journey. "Martin, I have to get to West Tisbury. It is a town near here. Can you help me find it?"

"I know someone who can help. She fishes in the harbor this time of night. I bet she will know how to get there."

Martin led the way off the ship. They crept along in the rockweed exposed at low tide. Lampposts near shore made pools of light on the still harbor water.

"Quiet now. That's her up ahead." A great blue heron, standing still as a statue, looked out at the water.

With a quick movement, she dipped her beak in the water. She stood back upright, dripping water. Her beak was empty. Turning toward the three animals, she said, "What do you want, Martin? You are disturbing my fishing."

"Good evening, Gretchen. My new friends need your help." She stared at them without blinking. The water lapped at the rocks at her feet. Nicholas felt uncomfortable in her gaze.

"I need to get to West Tisbury," Nicholas started. "Do you know where that is?" Gretchen continued to watch the small animals.

"Now see here," Edward piped up. "My friend needs some help. He needs to get to West Tisbury as soon as possible. Can you help him?"

"I know where it is. It's a town on an island called Martha's Vineyard. I might even take him there, but not right now," Gretchen said, looking at Nicholas.

"This is the best time for fishing." The heron waded back along the shore and stood looking out at the water.

Nicholas and Edward followed Martin up to the grass. "I can't believe we are finally going to get to West Tisbury, Edward. My uncle will be so surprised to see me."

"Nicholas, I won't be going with you," Edward said. "I am close to my home now. I live in the Myles Standish Forest, just to the west of town."

Nicholas looked at his friend. "You and I have been through so much, Edward. Don't you want to come along and meet my uncle?" Nicholas suddenly felt very lonely.

"My family will be expecting me for Thanksgiving." Edward cleared his throat a few times. "You are a true friend, Nicholas. I wouldn't have made it home without your help. Good-bye, Nicholas." Edward hugged his friend and scampered off across the grass heading for the forest and home.

Nicholas tried not to think of his friend heading off into the night. He sighed sadly, thinking that he was on his own again. Nicholas knew it would be a long time before he would be heading to his own home again.

Chapter Twenty-Five

Nicholas grew cold and tired waiting for Gretchen. He fell asleep leaning against Martin's soft fur. The great blue heron patiently plucked minnows out of the water until she had her fill. A light breeze ruffled the water. Nicholas awoke to the heron leaning over him, her gray eye close to his face. Martin had gone.

"We must go now," Gretchen said. "It will be dawn soon. You may climb onto my back and we will fly off." Nicholas scrambled up.

"I know all about flying," Nicholas said. "We hitched a ride with a Canada goose once."

"Hold on" is all Gretchen said. She leaped into the air. It was not like the long takeoff of a goose. One minute, the heron was standing on the ground, and the next minute she was airborne. Nicholas squeaked, held on to Gretchen's feathers, and tried to stay on her back. They flew along the coast, away from the ship.

It was still dark but the sky had become lighter. Nicholas could see streetlights in town. A few cars appeared on the roads.

"Plymouth looks like a pretty town," Nicholas said. Gretchen remained silent. She beat her great wings slowly. She followed a marshy river along the shore. Soon she set down on the riverbank in some cattails.

"Are we in West Tisbury already?" Nicholas asked. The sun was coming up. Nicholas could make out small houses made of bark under some trees, up away from the river.

"We are still in Plymouth," Gretchen said. "This area is the homeland of the Wampanoag People. They have lived here for thousands of years. They were here before the Pilgrims and named this area Patuxet.

"The Wampanoag lived along the coast in the summer. They grew corn, fished in the ocean, and hunted game in the forest," Gretchen said. "They view the earth and all of nature as a gift from the creator."

"Are the Wampanoag all gone?" Nicholas asked.

"No, many Wampanoag people live in this area today. They work hard keeping the old ways alive. Some work at a museum called Plimoth Plantation and they teach visitors about native ways." Gretchen grew silent. She and Nicholas watched the sun rise up over the cattails.

"Native people pass their family stories down through the generations. That's how they keep their history alive. There is a story about Martha's Vineyard the natives tell," Gretchen said.

"The island you are headed for was once called Capawock by the Wampanoag," Gretchen said. "Sometimes natives tell of a giant named Maushop, who lived long ago. He made his home along the shores of Cape Cod. He could stand with one foot in the bay and one foot in the ocean."

"Was he a fierce giant?" Nicholas asked.

"No, he watched out for natives living along the coast. He would bring them food when they were hungry and firewood for cooking. He fought a great bird, as big as an island, which was attacking native children."

"He created the landscape around Cape Cod," Gretchen said. "Maushop, walking through the water, collected sand in his moccasins. When he shook it out the sand formed the island of Martha's Vineyard. The smoke from his pipe comes back as fog along the shore."

"He had a wife named Squant, four sons, and a

beautiful daughter. A great stone marks where Squant stood near the mouth of a river. Their children turned into fish in the sea."

"What happened to Maushop? Is he still around?" Nicholas asked.

"The Wampanoag say that before the Europeans came, Maushop waded out into the water, turned into a white whale, and swam away."

Nicholas thought about the stories. He tried to imagine a world of giants and mysterious events. He wondered if his family journal had stories like that. He knew he was close to finding his uncle.

"Gretchen, will you take me to Martha's Vineyard? My family is counting on me to find my uncle and the journal of our family stories."

"Climb up, Nicholas, it is not far now. I will take you over the sea to Martha's Vineyard."

Gretchen leaped into the air and this time Nicholas was ready. He held tightly to the heron. He watched as they soared over cedar trees and cattail swamps heading away from the river. As they flew higher, Nicholas could see all of Cape Cod. Martha's Vineyard lay to the south.

As they approached the island, Nicholas could see boats in the harbor and sandy beaches. In the middle of the island, he saw small towns and country roads. Old stone walls marked out farm fields just like back home. Somewhere down there, Nicholas hoped he would find his uncle and the end of his journey.

Chapter Twenty-Six

Gretchen landed in a marshy spot near a town. He thanked the quiet bird for the ride.

"You may find help in town," she said, pointing toward a road. "I am off to visit cousins who live on the other side of the island." With that, she flew away.

Gretchen had brought Nicholas to a small town called Oak Bluffs. In the summer, visitors filled the streets and beaches. Now, in late November, Nicholas was alone. He sniffed along, looking for some food. He found a big wooden building with the words "Flying Horses" painted on the outside.

"What are you doing here? Are you lost?" Nicholas heard a voice say. A young girl in blue overalls bent over, looking at him. "Are you hungry?" she asked. She held out a bag of peanuts. Nicholas hid behind the bush, wary of the girl.

"It's all right, little fella. I won't hurt you." She shook the peanuts and backed away slowly. "Come here," she said, luring Nicholas out in to the open. He sniffed the air. She poured some out onto her hand. "Here you go."

Nicholas twitched his whiskers and stood on his hind legs. The girl called to him sweetly, "You don't have to be afraid." He ran to her and helped himself to the peanuts.

"There's plenty more inside. I'll put you in my pocket." The girl tucked Nicholas into the bib pocket of her overalls.

"There you are, Molly," a man with his own overalls said. He held a rag and big wrench in his hands. "I think I fixed the problem. Are you ready to take a test run?" Nicholas stayed hidden in Molly's pocket.

"Sure, Dad. Can I pick any horse?"

Nicholas heard circus music. Molly laughed and said, "Giddy up, Flash." Nicholas peeked out of the top of the pocket and saw that they were riding on a carousel of painted horses

137

hanging on chains. As the carousel spun around, the horses flew out in a big circle. Molly laughed again. "Hold on, little mouse, Flash can really fly."

Nicholas felt like he was flying high in the sky again. "You fixed it, Dad," Molly shouted as she passed her father.

The carousel slowed down, the horse hung down from the chains again, and the music stopped. Molly jumped off and ran to her father. "Look, Dad, I found him outside can I bring him home?" Nicholas wiggled in her hands.

Molly said, "He ate some peanuts right out of my hand. We'll have lots of fun at home." Nicholas wondered if they knew his uncle.

Molly and her father left the building. Her father called for their dog, Clyde. A slobbery old golden retriever jumped into the cab of the truck. They packed Nicholas in the back in an empty box with some peanuts and a rag to keep warm.

"You ride back here," Molly said. "I don't think you would get along with Clyde."

Nicholas watched trees and colorfully decorated houses whiz by. The truck traveled along the coast road and cruised into another town. They stopped near a bakery with a black dog painted on the sign. Nicholas jumped from the truck just as it took off again.

Nicholas wondered if his friend Tony was around. He wandered around to the back of the bakery. A large mouse wiggled backward out of a small hole.

"Thanks ever so much," the mouse said. "I'll see you again in a few weeks." The portly mouse held some bits of bread. His fur had a dusting of flour. "Ah, there's nothing like freshly baked bread. Would you care for some?" Nicholas ate a small piece.

"The old cat in the bakery and I go back a long way," the big mouse was saying. "We've been friends ever since I came back from my tour of New England. I had just been in Stockbridge, I believe. Anyway, one night he caught his paw in the big mixer and I helped him out. He gives me a little bread now and then."

"Did you say Stockbridge?" Nicholas asked. "That's where I'm from. I'm looking for my uncle William."

"That's my name," the big mouse said. "Are you young Nicholas? Well, bless my soul. Fancy meeting you here!"

"I've come a long way looking for you. Wait until you hear the adventures I've had." Nicholas dropped his bread and hugged his uncle. He was happy, excited, and tired after the long journey.

"Come with me, Nicholas. We have to hurry. You can tell me all about your trip on our way to my home."

Down the street a lanky man wearing a plaid shirt, green pants, and suspenders climbed into an old beat-up truck. The two mice ran toward it. The back of the truck held crates covered with canvas.

"Jump aboard, nephew. It's comfortable under the canvas." They hopped onto the truck as it roared to life. They found a quiet corner among the crates.

"Now, Nicholas, tell me why you have come all this way." William turned toward Nicholas. Nicholas had fallen fast asleep. The long journey and the excitement of finding his uncle at last were too much for the young mouse. The truck bounced along. William sat quietly next to Nicholas, who slept soundly with a small smile on his face.

Chapter Twenty-Seven

Nicholas awoke when the truck came to a stop in front of a red barn. For a few minutes, he thought he was home again. For a few minutes he thought all of his adventures had been a dream.

"Here we are, Nicholas. My home," Uncle William said. The farm was perched atop a hill. He could see the ocean off in the distance. He knew he wasn't home but he was glad his uncle was there.

William and Nicholas leaped from the truck and went into the barn. It was dark inside. It smelled of hay, animals, and spilled diesel fuel from the tractors.

"This was an old grist mill, years and years ago," William said. "They ground corn and wheat to make flour. Now it's a barn for cows and horses." The two mice climbed a set of wooden steps. Stacks of baled hay filled the space.

"This way, Nicholas," William climbed a ladder that leaned against the wall. They arrived in the very top of the barn in a small space full of old wooden gears and shafts. It was quiet there. The wind made the barn creak like an old ship. Off in the distance, the ocean surf pounded on the shore.

"This old loft makes a wonderful apartment." William offered Nicholas some apple seeds he had stashed away in the corner. "Now tell me what has brought you all the way from the other end of the state." Nicholas munched on his apple seeds, trying to decide where to begin.

"First, there was the rain and our house was flooded. The family journal was ruined." With that, the words flowed out. He told William about the old owl in the forest, meeting Edward, helping the beaver in Quabbin, fishing on the Grand Banks, and everything else along the way.

William listened silently. When Nicholas stopped, William sat for a few minutes looking at his amazing nephew.

"You have had quite an adventure, Nicholas. It reminds me of when I was young. I've seen all the states of New England and parts of New York, too.

I remember visiting your parents long ago. I made a copy of our journal and brought it home here with me. I kept it safe in my apartment for years."

"You know, Nicholas, our mouse family has not always lived in Massachusetts. At one time, there were no house mice in New England. Now there are many branches of our family all over," William said. "We traveled here with the first settlers. We came on ships and made our homes with the colonists. Your family can trace its line back to the very first ship to come to New England. And our journal tells the whole tale."

"I knew you would have it, Uncle William," Nicholas said. "Can I see it?" Nicholas was excited to hear about his family and he wanted to read all the details. William looked at Nicholas. William rolled his front paws together.

"I …" he started. "Well, you see, Nicholas …" he continued. "I had the journal for so long. I kept it safe and wrote in it sometimes but…" William stood up and paced back and forth across the room.

"It's not here, Nicholas," William said all at once. "Your cousin was here this summer. He wanted to copy the journal for family that lives in Maine. I let him take it home."

Nicholas jumped up. He could not believe it!

"I have traveled so far and been through so much. How can the journal not be here? My family is counting on me. I have to get home to help. They expect me to bring the journal home." He sat down with a thump. A puff of dust floated up in the air. The room seemed quieter than ever now.

William stood by a small knothole looking out and thinking. He turned, looking at his sad nephew. "Nicholas, what if you spend the winter here with me? I will tell you all the stories I know about our family."

Nicholas thought about what his uncle said. Nicholas had promised his parents he would come home with the journal, and he promised to come back to help them rebuild their home. He didn't know what to do. He wished Edward were here so they could talk over his problem. Edward would help him find a solution.

He looked over at his uncle, who was smiling at Nicholas and smoothing out his old gray whiskers. His uncle had been all over New England, Nicholas thought. If he could find his way around New England, then certainly, I can find my way to Maine, Nicholas reasoned. His uncle seemed to guess what Nicholas was thinking. "You are a lot like me, young Nicholas. Once you get the urge to travel, it's hard to stay at home, but you should stay with me through the winter. I will help you prepare for your trip north."

"Uncle William, I need to go to Maine to find my cousin and our family journal."

"Now Nicholas, this is no time of year for a little mouse to head off to Maine. In the spring, schooners stop here on their way back north. I will show you how to hitch a ride with them. Then I will go to Stockbridge to help your parents."

"Maine is a big state, Nicholas," his uncle said. "The coast is full of long winding peninsulas and islands. There are mountains and lakes in the west, trees stretching on for days and days in the north, big cities on rivers, and towns and small villages hidden in valleys. Nicholas, you will have many adventures in such a diverse state. You need to spend time with me so I can teach you how to find your way around."

Nicholas looked out the window near the peak of the barn. Small snowflakes had started to fall. It would be safe and warm for the winter here with his uncle. He could explore this island and spend time with his uncle. In the spring, when the warm sun and longer days came back, he would be ready to go off to Maine for more adventures. He would continue his search for the journal that tells the story of Nicholas and his family in New England.

Keeping a Journal

Throughout this story, Nicholas is trying to find his family journal. As the story says, there are many reasons that people keep journals. Some people write in a journal in order to recall events that happened to them. Other people write stories that others tell them in a journal in order to keep those memories alive. And then, some people write in a journal as a way to record their personal thoughts and feelings. In this activity, you can try your hand at journal writing.

In the first part of this activity, you will interview someone (preferably a family member) and write down their stories and memories in your journal, just like Nicholas's parents did for his family. You can either buy a journal or simply make one by stapling some paper together. Get ready to write!

Part 1:

As a way to begin your journal, you will need to find a family member or friend who lives nearby to interview. This person should be at least one generation older than you, if not more. It would be ideal to interview a grandparent or a great-grandparent.

Your job is to ask the following questions of the person chosen and transcribe their stories. To transcribe a story is to take notes or tape record what a person says and then write it down.

Let the following questions guide the creation of your family journal:

1. What is your name? Age? Place where you were born?

2. What was our town like when you were my age?

State flower
Mayflower

3. What kinds of things did you do for fun when you were my age?

4. Who were the important people in your life?

5. Were there any major historical events that took place when you were growing up?

6. Who were the members of the family that you grew up in? Are there any memorable stories about that family?

7. Tell a story about a very happy moment in your early life.

8. Tell a story about a sad or challenging time in your life.

9. Tell about where your family originally came from.

10. Tell about any other important memories/stories that should be included in this journal.

Hopefully after interviewing the person, you will have learned a great deal about the history of his family or the area in which you live. As you transcribe, remember that since this is your journal, you may add in your own feelings and reactions to the interview.

Part 2:

Next, you will begin the second half of your journal with your own entries. There are a couple of things to remember when writing your own journal entries. First, always remember to start with the date, including the year. This will be important in years to come when you or another family member look back at the entries. Also, when writing about people and places, make sure to include complete names (first and last if you are writing about a person). This will make it easier to recall memories in the future.

State bird
Black-capped
Chickadee

Throughout the story *Nicholas: A Massachusetts Tale*, many events happen that would make outstanding journal entries for Nicholas. In your journal, you can record the things that happen to you and the things you see on your adventures. If you need suggestions for things to write about, consider the list below to guide your journal entries.

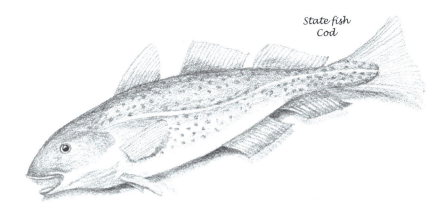

State fish
Cod

Write about a time…

1. when you were extremely brave.
2. when you had to solve a problem.
3. that you helped someone.
4. that you were very surprised.

Remember, this is just a list of possible journal topics, but what makes a journal truly unique is writing about whatever is important to you!

State tree
Elm

 mitten press

Mitten Press is proud to launch this series of chapter books about a lively field mouse from Massachusetts. He lives tucked under a farmhouse outside Stockbridge until a flood destroys the journal that contains his family history. Nicholas will embark on a journey across the state to locate his uncle who possesses another copy of the precious journal. On his travels, he'll make friends with a self-important chipmunk named Edward and learn a great deal about his home state.

The series will chronicle Nicholas's adventures throughout New England. In each book, young readers will learn about another state—the animals that live there, the geography, and even the state's history—as Nicholas continues his search for his family journal.

Coming soon …
Nicholas: A Maine Tale
ISBN: 978-1-58726-520-4

Join Nicholas's New England Readers by sending your email address to the publisher at ljohnson@mittenpress.com. You will receive updates as new books in the series are completed and fun activities to challenge what you know about the New England states.

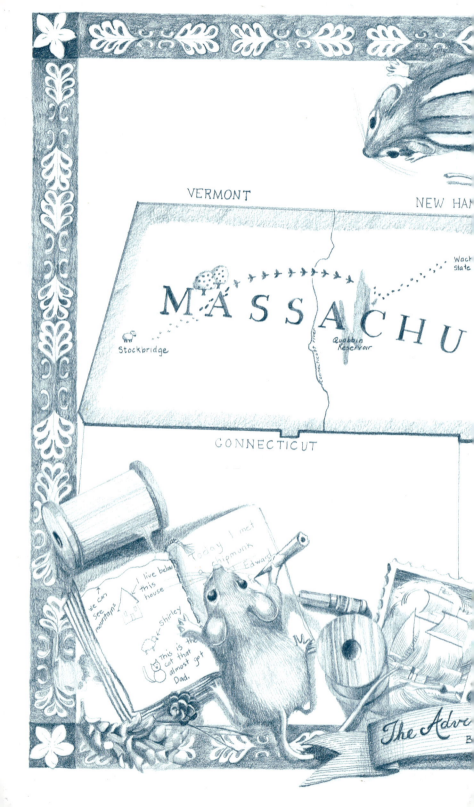